The Midnight Intruder

Gayle Roper

ACCENT BOOKS

Denver, Colorado

ACCENT BOOKS

A division of Accent Publications, Inc.
12100 West Sixth Avenue
P.O. Box 15337
Denver, Colorado 80215

Copyright © 1987 Accent Publications, Inc.
Printed in the United States of America

Library of Congress Catalog Card Number 86-73026

ISBN 0-89636-229-9

In gratitude for technical assistance:

Jim Davis. Director, City Gate, Coatesville, Pennsylvania

Barbara Grubbs, piano teacher, Parkesburg, Pennsylvania

Tony Harley, former police officer, Tredyffrin Police Department, Tredyffrin, Pennsylvania

Linda B. Marshall, M.D., Brandywine Hospital, Coatesville, Pennsylvania

Sgt. Charles O'Donnell, Coatesville Police Department, Coatesville, Pennsylvania

1

Geoff McGregor pulled on his tattered running shorts and T-shirt, whistling through his teeth as he listened to Sandi Patti play in his ear. He tied his jogging shoes and clipped his Walkman to his belt.

It was a beautiful night, perfect for running. The mid-June day had been unbearable, but a light breeze had come from somewhere, and now the humidity was negligible.

At the door, Geoff stopped and considered the wisdom of running so late. He looked at his watch. Eleven p.m. on a June Thursday. If he were still in Philadelphia, he'd never consider running at such an hour. But this was the country.

The night was too much to resist. He started down the hill to the reservoir and the road that encircled it. After years of running through the city's pollution and exhaust fumes, the fresh country air smelled marvelous.

His feet slap-slapped against the macadam, but he didn't hear the sound. Sandi's sweet and powerful vocals swam through his mind.

Geoff smiled happily. He was enjoying his two weeks of relaxation and total solitude, unless he counted Abraham, a Newfoundland who thought he was a lap dog, and Teensie, a hamster who made an incredible amount of noise on that Machiavellian running wheel of hers.

He was glad he had resisted his sister's invitation to join their vacation in Ocean City.

"Come to the shore with us the last two weeks of June," Janie had said at the family Memorial Day picnic, held on the first weekend in June because Geoff had had to work the holiday weekend. "You can enjoy the beach and the sun, and the kids would love to have Uncle Geoff around."

Geoff had looked at his sister and brother-in-law, two nephews and one niece and smiled. He dearly loved all five of them, but two weeks at the shore sharing showers, sand and mosquito bites wasn't his idea of relaxation.

Without rancor and with understanding, Arch had silently handed Geoff the key to their home just west of East Edge in beautiful, rural Chester County, Pennsylvania. Geoff had taken it gratefully. The house was a real luxury after the cramped city apartments he had lived in over the years of his study at Hahnamann University Hospital and Children's Hospital of Philadelphia.

Janie and Arch's house sat on a hill overlooking a golf course and reservoir. Before he left, Arch got Geoff a guest pass for the course and left his golf clubs for his brother-in-law, a sure sign of the esteem he had for Geoff.

The reservoir itself was edged on two sides with homes, some very elegant, some merely attractive. A third side was heavily wooded, providing a home for raccoons, opposum, skunks, numerous birds, various rodents, and a few brave deer. The fourth side of the reservoir shore was bordered by the golf course. The path paralleled the shore just a few yards into the tree line.

Geoff circled the reservoir once, a distance of three miles, and decided to do it again. The emptiness of the night felt so relaxing. An occasional car passed along the road, throwing a faint gleam on the fluorescent stripes of his sneakers and the worn fluorescent letters on his T-shirt that read "Joggers are God's people" on both front and back.

Geoff sang along mentally with Sandi. He was puffing too much to do anything else. A great feeling of exhilaration and accomplishment filled him. His residency was now behind him, the future beckoned brightly, and he still had most of his two week vacation yet to enjoy.

Enveloped in his wave of euphoria, Geoff almost missed the activity at the edge of the reservoir where the golf course fell away into deserted blackness. A brief stab of light caught his eye.

Slowing down, he peered through the darkness. Huge pines rimmed the reservoir and a car had been backed up between them to the water's edge. Its trunk was open. The stab of light that had drawn Geoff's attention must have been the trunk light before someone disconnected it.

He slid his earphones off, fumbled with the controls to turn Sandi off, and stood listening, trying to hear over the noise of his own breathing. Two men were silhouetted blackly against the pale gray gleam of the water as they stood whispering.

Geoff remembered Janie's stories of jewelry that his nephews, Zach and Tim, had dug up once when the

7

reservoir's water level was very low. The treasure was the worthless stuff left from robberies, the things that couldn't be fenced, good only to be thrown in the water and sink forever out of sight.

Geoff watched the men reach in the trunk and pull out something large and cumbersome. It took him only a minute to know it was a body.

His scalp prickled. He began to back away one cautious step at a time when he stepped on a branch. It cracked like a shot under his weight.

The two men dropped their bundle with a splash and spun around.

"What's that?" one of them shouted. "Is somebody there?"

"Shut up," hissed the second. "It's probably just an animal."

A flashlight beam cut the darkness and found the fluorescent letters on Geoff's T-shirt. The light moved immediately to his face.

He threw himself sideways even as a shot tore the silence. He felt a hot searing against his left forehead. He blinked in disbelief. He'd been shot!

"Did you get him?" he heard the first man ask.

"I don't know. Go see."

Pressing against a large tree trunk, Geoff shook his head to clear it. His ears rang from the buffeting of the air displacement, but he felt no particular pain except a burning where the bullet had creased his skull. He gently touched the wound and discovered that although he was bleeding profusely, it was neither deep nor dangerous.

A crashing through the underbrush indicated his pursuer's rapid approach. Geoff pulled off his shoes with their fluorescent stripes and threw them as far to his left as he could, hoping to misdirect the man.

The flashlight beam swerved immediately as did the direction of the thrashing.

Pulling his shirt with its giveaway letters off over his head, Geoff dodged from pine to pine, moving as quickly as he could away from the danger. The lights of a few houses still blinked tantalizingly even at this hour, a diamond chain reflected in myriad sparkles on the water. Their gleam meant safety, but he knew the closest ones were a mile away.

Geoff looked back over his shoulder when he heard a voice call, "It's only his sneakers."

He took a deep breath and tried to move faster. But his wound was beginning to throb, and his head felt huge and heavy on his shoulders. Geoff used his balled up shirt to mop at the blood that ran down his cheek and ear, then pressed it against the wound as hard as he could. Soon, he knew, he'd begin to feel weak and lightheaded from loss of blood.

His progress under the pines and through the scrubby undergrowth was slow and painful. Stones, pine cones, and thistles under his shoeless feet were one kind of agony; the branches and vines that scratched his chest and back were another. The open road was tempting, but he knew he'd be too visible. He plunged on, at least partially hidden, the houses drawing slowly nearer.

He stopped for a moment and listened. Sure enough, he heard the none too stealthy movements of his trackers. Suddenly the flashlight beam cut the night again. The light played slowly from right to left as the tracker sought his quarry. Geoff glued himself to a tree trunk as the light panned by him. He didn't understand why he was worth chasing, but obviously he was. Could they fear he had seen them well enough to identify them?

Maybe he should yell, "Hey, guys, I never saw you! Honest!"

Then again, maybe they thought he was a friend of the body's come to take revenge, and they'd better get him first.

When the beam cut toward the reservoir's edge, Geoff took a deep breath and ran across the road toward the first house. His back twitched as he anticipated a bullet. He had never felt so vulnerable.

He stumbled through a great mass of pachysandra, across a yard, and crouched in the shrubbery of a contemporary cedar shake house. Only then did he realize that the house was empty. Dismay floored him. He'd assumed that the first house meant safety.

As his pursuer turned toward the road, Geoff decided that his greatest chance for safety lay in threading through backyards until he came to an inhabited house. Then he'd just bang on the back door until someone came to help.

Leaving the cover of the bushes that bordered the house, he raced for a large holly at the far edge of the property. If he could get behind it unnoticed, he could reach the backyard of the next house with no problem. But when he dove behind the holly, he found a tall, impenetrable spike fence circling the backyard.

Assessing his options hurriedly, he knew he'd have to run across the driveway and the front lawn to the third house. With each property almost an acre in size, the yards were immense.

But Geoff also knew he wouldn't be able to keep moving much longer. His vision kept blurring, and his head felt like a medicine ball on his shoulders. His chest was sticky with lost blood, and his breath rasped harshly.

As he lurched across the driveway, his feet slapped the macadam softly. Whether it was that slight noise or his movement, he didn't know, but something attracted the attention of the hunter. Geoff heard him cross the street and saw the flashlight scan the yard he had just crossed.

As Geoff threw himself around the far corner of the second house, its front porch light suddenly illuminated the yard. Pinned in the brilliance like a deer was the hunter. In his right hand was a small gun.

Blinking his eyes, Geoff stared at the man, trying to focus so he could identify him later. But his brain was too foggy to sort out the images it was receiving.

The man threw himself to the ground as the front door opened and, a little dog about the size of Teensie, Zach and Tim's hamster, scampered out, barking happily.

"Now, hurry, Tidbit, do your duty," called a rather obese man. "Daddy wants to go to bed."

Geoff couldn't control a smirk as the yipping dog ran unerringly to the man lying in his front yard. The animal's master might never see the man recumbent on his lawn, lost in the shadows of the night, but for Geoff, the little dog was as good as a squadron of Marines.

Geoff moved carefully and painfully on past the darkened third house and was halfway across the backyard of the fourth when the sliding glass patio door suddenly opened. A hand reached out to shake some placemats.

Instinctively Geoff flattened himself against the brickwork behind a full and fragrant clematis vine. He realized immediately that stopping had not been wise. All his pricks and pains shouted at him in dissonant chorus. Lightheadedness made him woozy. Here was his chance to ask for help, and he seemed unable to move.

Suddenly two cats charged across the patio and skidded to a halt in the grass almost in front of him. A woman's voice called them. When they wouldn't respond, she began chasing them with no success.

A car door slammed out front, scaring the cats into the house. The noise also made Geoff jump, and a wave of nausea swept over him. He staggered forward as the dizziness affected his balance.

Through blurred eyes, he saw the woman staring at him in fear.

"Don't be afraid," he said hoarsely.

He wasn't certain the words were loud enough for her to hear, so he repeated them. "Don't be afraid."

"What do you want?" she asked, her voice reflecting her fear.

He jerked his head toward the house. He knew he had to lie down before he fell down. But the quick movement was a mistake, and he grabbed his head to keep it from falling off.

"You're hurt!" she exclaimed, moving quickly toward him.

Geoff stepped backward in reaction to her sudden approach. As he did so, he trod on something that moved beneath his feet, and he began falling.

2

Jenna Mathisson stared at the large man bleeding onto her patio. What in the world should she do? Call the police? An ambulance? A doctor?

Tommy, why aren't you here when I need you?

She was instantly ashamed of blaming her dead husband for her predicament and fear. In a way it was his fault that she lived alone in this isolated house with only two small children for company. If Tommy were here as he was supposed to be, she wouldn't be so vulnerable. She'd be screaming her lungs out for his help. But it helped no one, least of all her, to throw blame at him for a situation beyond repair. Two years was a long time, and she'd thought she was doing so well in dealing with her feelings toward him.

Still staring at the fallen giant she saw his eyelids flutter, and felt great relief. He groaned and stirred, as she knelt beside him.

"Are you all right?"

What a stupid question, Jenna. He is obviously not all right. All right men don't bleed, have their bare chests all

13

scratched up, and wear torn, dirty socks with no shoes.

He groaned again and tried to sit up, but his body wouldn't respond completely to the command his mind gave it. He ended up leaning on one elbow, his head buried in his hand.

"I'd better call you a doctor," Jenna told the top of his head.

"Don't bother," he said weakly. "I'm fine."

"No, you're not. You need your injuries looked at. I'd take you to the hospital, but I can't leave my kids alone."

"I don't need a doctor," he repeated stubbornly. "I *am* a doctor."

"Oh."

Jenna studied him. He certainly didn't look like a doctor. He looked more like the losing boxer after a knockout.

"Were you in an accident?"

"No. I was shot."

Jenna blinked. "Oh."

She looked blankly at the cats who stared back at her from the safety of the family room. Then suddenly her back began to prickle. She hastily placed it against the house and scanned the trees that rimmed the back-yard.

"What do you mean you were shot? Who shot you? Are they chasing you? Are they still out there? And I was upset about the cats escaping! Get up, will you? We've got to get inside!"

Jenna reached out to him and began to drag him to his feet. He tried to cooperate.

"I don't know who they are or where they are," he mumbled as he lurched upright, gasping as he leaned

14

against the door to prevent collapse.

"Don't bother leaning out here," Jenna ordered, her ears straining to hear any noises made by unseen assassins. "You can lean inside."

She got behind the man and pushed him through the door. As soon as they were inside, she whirled around and slammed the door shut. Ramming the burglar bar home and pulling the drapes, she left him rocking as she raced around the house, shutting all the curtains and turning off all the lights but the one in the kitchen.

Hurrying back to the injured man who was leaning against the wall holding his head, she suddenly thought, *What have I done! I've locked myself in my own house with a strange man!* Every newspaper article she'd ever read about foolish women being attacked rushed to jumbled recall.

Don't let them know you're afraid, she remembered. *No, that was animals, but maybe it would work with men, too.* Since she couldn't very well dump him back on the patio, she had no choice but to find out. *Lord,* she breathed in a quick prayer, *I need your help.*

Pushing the man down onto a kitchen chair, Jenna's eye caught the phone. She quickly picked it up, dialed, and spoke into the receiver.

"Here." She thrust the phone at the man. "It's the police. Tell them what happened."

Thankful for the sudden inspiration, Jenna gathered a bowl of warm water, some washcloths, disinfectant, and a blanket as he talked. When he hung up, she began to clean his face gingerly.

"They'll be here quite soon, I should imagine," the man said, beginning to shiver with shock.

"I certainly hope so," said Jenna. "How did you manage to get yourself shot?" She wrapped a blanket about his shoulders.

"I don't know. I was just jogging around the reservoir."

Jenna's eyes opened wide in surprise. "Isn't it a bit late for jogging?" The clock showed almost midnight.

"I thought it was safe in the country," he defended.

"Weird people live in the country, too," Jenna said unnecessarily. "The reservoir is never the safest place after dark, though usually the couples who go there to park, drink or do dope don't bother people. They want privacy."

Still strange things did happen. One night a girl had come to the Mathisson door because the light was on. She had driven to the reservoir with some friends for a midnight swim and gotten scared for some reason. Tommy had driven her home.

Another time at 4:00 a.m. on a bitter winter Saturday morning, a couple with an appreciable amount of gray hair on their heads had come to the door nearly frozen. They had gotten stuck in a snow drift, and had tried to get themselves out for several hours until they ran out of gas. Then, fearful of the deadly cold, they had gone looking for a light and found the Mathissons'. Tommy had driven them home, too.

But a shooting was a new and unpleasantly violent occurrence.

Jenna stepped back to look at the injured man. "It's mostly just blood," she told him. "Just two scalp wounds, a good sized egg in the back where you hit when you fell over Mikey's truck and one from your bullet."

He looked at her and smiled weakly. "Thanks, whoever you are."

"Jenna Mathisson."

"I'm Geoff McGregor. Maybe you know my sister and brother-in-law, Janie and Arch Steager? They live just up the hill."

Jenna felt the relief physically; her shoulders fell about three inches as the tension left. Many times she had heard Janie talk about her brother-the-doctor, and Zach, Tim, and Patsy were always talking about Uncle Geoff.

Just then the doorbell rang, and Jenna went quickly to answer it. There were two policemen, a lieutenant with a craggy face and a patrolman who looked like he was just out of the police academy. Both were in uniform.

Jenna took them into the kitchen. The police lieutenant looked unhappy, as well he might. Night duty in East Edge was usually quiet. Now he had a body in the reservoir and an attempted murder victim in—the lieutenant looked again—running shorts, tattered socks, and a blanket.

He ran his hand through his brown curls and blinked his bloodshot eyes a few times. When he thought no one was looking, he popped a Tums.

The young patrolman was fairly bursting with enthusiasm. Jenna thought it was probably his first real case. East Edge was generally a very peaceful town.

"So you're the one who called?" the lieutenant asked Geoff.

Geoff nodded, felt his head begin to spin and said, "Yes."

"You say you saw men dumping a body in the reservoir?" Skepticism fairly dripped from his tongue.

Geoff and Jenna both looked at him in surprise.

"I most definitely did see men dumping a body in the reservoir," said Geoff with asperity. "I know a body when I see one."

"You do? A dead body?"

"I'm a doctor, Lt. Whateveryournameis."

"Lt. Janczyn. And this is Patrolman Monihan." The last was a throwaway. Obviously the lieutenant didn't expect much from the patrolman.

"I'm a doctor, Lt. Janczyn," repeated Geoff. "Dr. Geoffrey L. McGregor. I know a body when I see one."

"May I see your identification, Doctor?"

Geoff reached for his hip pocket only to realize he had nothing that could identify him. "I don't have any with me."

The lieutenant looked at Jenna. "Perhaps Mrs. McGregor has some identification?"

Jenna flushed and stammered, "I'm n-not Mrs. McGregor. My name is Jenna Mathisson, and this is my house. Dr. McGregor came here when he was being chased."

Lt. Janczyn looked at Jenna with interest, and she flinched slightly under the scrutiny. She knew the hoopla aroused when Tommy Mathisson and his family had bought a house on the East Edge reservoir. Unconsciously she rubbed suddenly sweaty palms over her apricot slacks, unaware of the smear of blood on the left leg.

"And you can vouch for this man?" the lieutenant said to her. "You know him?"

"I just met Dr. McGregor tonight," she said.

"And you let him into your house?" Lt. Janczyn's tone was critical.

"He was unconscious on my patio. He was being

chased by somebody with a gun. What was I to do? Let him lie there and bleed to death? Let him get killed?"

"How do you know there was anyone chasing him?" the lieutenant asked.

Jenna thought for a moment. The policeman had raised a good question. How did she know?

"I don't *know* there was someone chasing him," she finally said, "but I do know he was shot. See?" She pointed to the angry welt over Geoff's left temple.

Lt. Janczyn nodded. "There's no doubt he was shot, and there's no doubt he's one fortunate man. I guess my problem is that I don't understand why anyone would get involved in a shooting at the reservoir in the middle of the night without something funny going on."

"But there was something funny going on," Geoff said. "There was a body being thrown in the reservoir."

"And you just happened to wander by?"

"Yes!" replied Geoff angrily. "I just happened to wander by. I went jogging, foolishly thinking that the country was safe, even at that late hour. How wrong I was! I never ran into anything like this in all my years in inner city Philadelphia. Just here in your jurisdiction."

Lt. Janczyn rose, his eyes frosty. "I'd like you to come with me and show me where you saw this supposed occurrence. The shore line out there is so big, it'd take us hours to find this body without your help."

"Glad to, Lieutenant." Geoff rose shakily to his feet.

"Does he have to go?" Jenna asked in concern. "He's hurt!"

"Yes, he does. And I'll take good care of him," said the lieutenant.

As everyone walked to the door, Patrolman Monihan

19

leaned toward Jenna. "Don't mind the lieutenant. He's grouchy when he works night duty. And he's probably got an ulcer that he won't admit to."

"Do tell," said Jenna. But she felt a bit better. At least half of their police relationship wasn't adversarial. Patrolman Monihan seemed very nice.

"Are you coming back here?" she asked at the door.

"Who?" asked the lieutenant. "The good doctor? Or all of us?"

"All of you," said Jenna coldly. "I want to know whether I should wait up or go to bed."

"You can go to bed," he answered. "We'll take him into town for questioning."

Jenna looked at Geoff, swaying and pasty.

"No," she said. "Come back here. It'll be more comfortable and closer to home for him."

The lieutenant shrugged. "Fine by me. I'll need to talk with you again anyway."

They were back in less than twenty minutes. Jenna had barely had time to make some iced tea, check on her still sleeping children, and cut a coffee cake. As the men walked to the kitchen, she noticed Geoff running his hand along the wall for support.

He obviously felt vindicated. They had found the body almost immediately.

"It wasn't hard to find, really," Patrolman Monihan said excitedly while Lt. Janczyn talked on the phone. "It floated real well because it hadn't been in the water long enough to get waterlogged."

"Great," said Jenna as she swallowed.

"Pete," Lt. Janczyn said to his partner after he got off

20

the phone, "I want you to go back to the reservoir and wait for the troops. They'll be arriving as soon as they wake up enough to drive without killing themselves. Get started on identifying the body just as soon as you can."

Patrolman Monihan's smile was megawatt as he let himself out.

3

"Okay, Dr. McGregor," said Lt. Janczyn after Monihan had gone, "take it from the top. Tell me what happened tonight. Be as thorough as you can. Tell me anything, no matter how insignificant it seems."

Geoff took a drink of iced tea and began talking. Jenna listened with fascinated horror as Geoff related his escape through the underbrush along the edge of the reservoir.

"I was fine until I stepped on that stick," he finished. "Then, wham! They were after me."

"They had no idea who you were. You could have been very dangerous to them," the lieutenant pointed out.

"I thought about that as I was running. For all they knew, I was the body's buddy come to even the score."

"Why didn't you get lost in the darkness of the golf course?" asked the lieutenant.

"Because I thought the houses offered greater safety and help. I don't live around here, and I don't know how the golf course is laid out. I could see the houses. I knew help was there."

"You don't live around here, but you were jogging

around our reservoir in the middle of the night?" The lieutenant shook his head. "I may seem awfully suspicious, but I don't understand."

Geoff nodded and pointed in the general direction of Steagers'. "I'm staying at my sister and brother-in-law's home at the top of the hill while they're at the shore."

"And they are?"

"Janie and Arch Steager. 110 Hilltop Road."

"And you have a phone number where they can be reached?"

"Back at the house. Also, for identification purposes, you might contact Dr. Ben Rosell. I'm going to be his associate."

Lt. Janczyn looked at Geoff. "My kids went to Dr. Rosell. At least this information won't be difficult to verify."

The lieutenant munched on a piece of Jenna's coffee cake while he thought. He finished with a glass of iced tea and another Tums.

"Did you by any chance see the guys who chased you?"

"Yes and no," said Geoff. "A couple of doors down, I had just run across the yard when the front light suddenly came on. I looked back around the corner of the house, and there was the man who was chasing me, caught in the light."

The lieutenant looked almost happy.

Geoff continued. "The trouble is that I don't remember what I saw. All I know is that I saw a man. I was so worn out, and my head was so woozy that I literally wasn't seeing straight. I'm afraid I can't give you any kind of description."

The lieutenant sighed and ate another Tums.

"The man was only there a minute," Geoff continued. "Then he threw himself on the ground. The yard is so big that he looked like just a bump in the lawn. The man who came to the door to let his dog out could never have seen him lying there. But the dog did." Geoff grinned. "The dog ran right to him and began barking."

"Tidbit," said Jenna as she poured more iced tea in Lt. Janczyn's glass.

Geoff nodded. "That's what the man called him. Tidbit."

"So this Tidbit pinned the man down while you escaped?" The lieutenant looked skeptical.

"At that point," said Geoff, "all help was gladly received."

"Tidbit is a mouthy little thing," said Jenna. "If you didn't want to be found, you wouldn't want Tidbit around."

"As I ran on, I could hear the dog's owner calling, 'Come to Daddy, Tidbit. Come to Daddy. You're making too much noise.'"

"So you ran here and passed out on Mrs. Mathisson's back porch. And you," he turned to Jenna, "just happened to notice him lying there."

"No," said Jenna. "I was outside chasing the cats when a car door slammed. The noise scared the cats in and made Geoff jump. He was hiding in the clematis vine. He stepped on my son's truck, lost his footing, and hit his head when he fell."

"Let me recap," said Lt. Janczyn to Geoff. "You went jogging in the middle of the night, saw men throwing a body in the reservoir, got shot by these same men, ran with them pursuing, got rescued by a dog named Tidbit, got knocked unconscious because of a kid's truck, and were nursed by a beautiful woman you'd never met before."

Geoff grinned. It sounded absolutely ridiculous. But his rotation in the Emergency Room while at Hahnamann had taught him that ridiculous was par for the course.

"You've got it absolutely right," he said.

"I can't wait to tell the boys at the station. But tell me," said the lieutenant, switching gears. "The car door you heard slam, what was that? This is a secluded area. Night traffic is minimal. That noise may be significant."

"I've thought about it," said Geoff. "I have only the fuzziest recollection of the slam, but doesn't it make sense that the guy who stayed at the reservoir to dispose of the body was coming to collect the guy who was chasing me?"

"Doesn't it make equal sense that the first guy had come to join the second in the search for you? That instead of a reprieve, the noise could have signaled double danger?"

Jenna remembered the prickly sensation she had felt all the way up her spine when Geoff had told her he had been shot. She had just ascribed the sensation to nerves. But maybe someone had been watching them!

"But surely even scared or angry men realize that you can't go tearing around a neighborhood hunting someone without being noticed?" queried Geoff.

"By your logic and mine, you're right. But these dirtbags are hard to figure."

Lt. Janczyn rose from his chair. "I want to go see what's happening at the reservoir. I don't think I trust Monihan. He's too enthusiastic.

"I'll need to see you tomorrow, Dr. McGregor. At that

time you will please bring some identification with you. We'll talk again and walk through your experience. Ten sharp at the police station. Right now, I'd suggest a good night's sleep."

Geoff nodded wearily.

Jenna and the lieutenant moved to the front door. She watched the lieutenant drive away, then returned to the kitchen.

"Thanks for your help," Geoff said. He rose with effort, holding onto the table for support. "I'll get out of your way now."

Jenna looked out her back window in the direction of Janie and Arch's house. It was a good mile away, all uphill. There seemed to her no way Geoff could manage that walk. Then, too, whoever shot him might still be out there looking for him in spite of the police presence in the area.

Of course, she could drive him home, but she didn't like the idea of leaving the kids alone, even for so short a time.

What they should have done was ask Lt. Janczyn to drive Geoff home. Unfortunately, solutions after the situation helped no one.

"You oughtn't to be alone tonight, you know," she said, looking at Geoff's pale face. "What if you're concussed?"

"I'll manage," he said, shrugging.

"Why don't you spend the night here? You can use the guest room. I'll give you a bell you can ring if you need help—which you probably won't."

He looked at her. "You don't know me from Adam."

She nodded in agreement. "But I do know Janie and Arch. Their Tim is in Mikey's first grade class; we go to the same church, and I've frequently heard Janie talk about her brother, the doctor. Also, Lt. Janczyn knows you're here. Besides," she chuckled slightly, "from the looks of you, I'd be safe even if you were the attacker instead of the victim."

Jenna took Geoff to the guest room. It wasn't until she turned on the light that she remembered how many of Tommy's things were stuck in here so she wouldn't see them. The bureau was lined with trophies and inscribed footballs. Framed photos rested in stacks against the wall.

She tried to ignore them as she made up the bed. Geoff was too preoccupied staring in the mirror at the welt raised by the bullet to really see the room's treasures. But tomorrow he'd notice. She was certain of it. She sighed.

She rummaged in one of the bureau drawers and found a pair of Tommy's old shorts and a T-shirt, both reading "Property of the EAGLES."

"Here," she said, handing them to Geoff. "When you wash up, you can change into these."

She hurried from the room before he had a chance to comment. She didn't want to talk about the man who had worn those clothes.

4

Even though it was almost two in the morning, Jenna seated herself at her piano, ready to relieve her tension as she usually did, when she realized she couldn't play. Geoff McGregor needed his sleep.

Jenna lowered the cover over the keys of the grand piano and rose quickly, her sudden movement disturbing Lump and Midget as they slept side by side on the plush carpet. They looked at her accusingly, blinked their great green eyes, and returned to sleep.

Jenna eyed the cats jealously. Pampered creatures! If she could get half the sleep they got, maybe she wouldn't feel so tired all the time. She made a face at the animals.

"If it weren't for you two trying to run away, I'd never have gotten into this mess, you know."

They ignored her.

She bent down and patted Lump who began to purr happily. She remembered the day when they found the two little kittens at the playground, apparently dropped by someone who knew a foolish, softhearted mother like Jenna would come along and adopt them.

"He looks just like a lump of coal," Mikey had said of the animal. "He's so black. I think I'll name him that."

"Name him what, Mikey? Blackie?"

Mikey shook his head. "Lump. I'm going to name him Lump."

"You aren't."

"I am."

And Lump he had become.

Midget stretched, yawned and walked to Jenna, pushing Lump aside and demanding equal scratching time. Jenna enjoyed Midget, easily the biggest cat she'd ever seen. How the little striped gray kitten with the white blaze had grown into this affectionate monster was a mystery. Every night Midget slept with Jenna, curled up right in the center of Tommy's pillow.

She looked around the living room, barren of all furniture except one chair and the piano. She tried to recall the furniture that had filled the room, but as usual, she could remember only the colors. She knew there'd been a striped sofa in shades of blue, mauve and cream, but she couldn't see the pattern in her mind anymore. She remembered that it had pleased her aesthetically as it sat on the slate blue carpet and against the mauve drapes, but its particulars escaped her memory.

Much as Tommy's face escaped her memory.

She sighed deeply and wandered out to the kitchen and the dinner mess left from hours ago when the second wave of piano students had begun. The "after soup group," Mikey called them.

She began rinsing the dishes. Mikey's entire dinner went down the disposal. He must be the only kid on earth who didn't like spaghetti—unless it was Spaghetti-O's.

She sighed again. The kid would eat practically nothing. He was going to die of starvation right under her nose. They'd come and take her away and charge her with child abuse, all because she had a six-year-old genius who refused to eat.

In her hurry, she banged Libby's Snoopy glass against the sink. Relief surged through her when it didn't break and she knew she wouldn't have to explain to her three-year-old where her special glass had gone.

Pressing the heat miser button firmly because she couldn't afford to let the heat cycle run, Jenna started the dishwasher and went to collect the placemats lying in a ball outside on the patio where she'd dropped them when Geoff appeared.

She reached to open the drapes, recalled the blood on Geoff's face, and let the cord fall. There was no way she was going to go back outside tonight.

Her reflection stared back at her from the mirror beside the door. She was startled at the dark circles under her eyes. Maybe it was just mascara.

She rubbed the delicate flesh beneath her eyes. The smudges remained. She looked at herself critically. Her variegated blonde waves suited her open face. Her well-arched brows and thick lashes accented her blue eyes, and her nose turned up slightly above a gentle mouth and a firm chin. She was going to be thirty in a couple of months. Did she look older? Tired and worn from her emotional seesaws?

She made a face at herself and turned away, forcing herself to walk through the house to check doors and windows, making certain everything was all right so she could go to bed. She had to get some sleep. Tomorrow was a busy day and Saturday was the recital.

Her checkbook and statement were still on the desk in the family room. She stopped and looked at the figures, hoping that somehow they had changed since she last saw them. She pushed the keys on her calculator. The same numbers appeared, as immutable as death.

How was she ever going to buy Libby new sneakers? Or get Mikey the baseball mitt he wanted? And she'd noticed a jagged rip in her raincoat the last time she'd worn it. And the hot water faucet in the kids' bathroom was leaking. And the washer was making an awful grinding noise. And. And. And.

She buried her face in her hands.

Father, how am I going to manage? So many of my piano students drop lessons for the summer, and I barely feed us with a full roster.

She looked around the family room. It was a large airy room with large expanses of glass, all presently curtained against the threat of criminals outside. The furnishings were expensive, comfortable, Tommy's choice. The plush grays and muted roses were so relaxing to look at, and the chairs and sofas were so comfortable to sit in. How much longer would she be able to keep from selling the room bare?

In fact, how much longer would she be able to keep the house? If she were honest with herself, she knew she was fighting a losing and probably foolish battle. Soon her house would have to go, just like so many other things in her life had.

The first Christmas Tommy was gone, she'd sold the living room furniture so the kids could have a good holiday. The second year she'd sold Tommy's stereo system, compact disc player and tape deck. The silver BMW had gone early, too, to help pay Tommy's debts and so had the pool table and the sterling silver. Was the family room next? And then the house?

Everybody said she should sell the house. But it was her home! It used to be that the very thought of selling it and finding another, cheaper place was more than she could handle. It was probably a sign of healing that the thought no longer made her nauseous, merely infinitely sad.

God, give me wisdom.

She looked in one last time on the kids. Mikey lay tangled in his sheet. She straightened it and bent to kiss his forehead.

May he grow up with a heart for you, Lord.

Libby lay neatly on her back, her covers still primly tucked around her shoulders. She looked as if she hadn't moved a muscle since Jenna tucked her in more than five hours ago.

Protect her from any more chaos, Lord, so she may be emotionally healthy for your service.

Jenna moved on into her room and dropped wearily into bed. That night she dreamed of Tommy for the first time in a long time. Tommy leaping for a pass. Tommy hugging Gus Glassman, his coach. Tommy driving his red Porsche. Tommy praying. Tommy drunk. Tommy dead.

5

Jenna woke to the sounds of the kids bursting into her room that morning.

"Mom!" hissed Mikey. "There's a man asleep in the guest room!"

He and Libby clambered onto Jenna's bed and poked her to make certain she was awake.

"A man, Mom," repeated Libby.

Jenna nodded sleepily as she pulled herself up on one elbow. "I know."

Midget climbed off his pillow and onto Libby's lap. As the little girl patted him absently, he purred in contentment.

"Where'd he come from?" asked Mikey. "Who is he?"

Jenna yawned. It had been a very long and restless night.

"His name is Dr. McGregor, and he needed a place to sleep because he hurt his head. He's Tim's and Patsy's and Zach's uncle."

Good as Geoff's credentials were, when the kids sat at

the breakfast table, they stared at him uncertainly. They hadn't seen a man here for a long time, and when they had, the situation had been exceedingly unpleasant.

"Have you any aspirin?" Geoff asked as he drank some orange juice. "I have a roaring headache."

"Thank God that's all you have," said Jenna as she left the room to get some.

She returned to find Mikey standing trembling beside the table, looking daggers at Geoff.

"I don't like to talk about *him*," the boy said and stalked off.

"Easy, Tiger," Jenna said, resting her hand on his shoulder as he passed. "It's all over, remember?"

The boy stopped and nodded, still looking grim.

"I love you. Libby loves you. And Daddy loved you."

Mikey snorted. "How do you know?"

Jenna wondered how many times they had had this conversation and how many more times they'd have it before Mikey grew up. "I know because he told me."

Mikey shook his head and walked to his room. Jenna let him go.

"All I said was how lucky he was to have had a father as special as Tommy Mathisson," Geoff said, looking so distressed that Jenna had to smile in spite of her concern for Mikey.

Jenna shrugged. "Things weren't too good Tommy's last year or two," she said in massive understatement. "Mikey remembers too well."

"My Daddy played football," said Libby proudly. Her memory of Tommy was essentially non-existent, a fact for which Jenna was both thankful and sorry. "He was an Eagle."

"And a very fine one," said Geoff. "I saw him play both in person and on TV."

Libby smiled at him and left the table to watch television.

"My years at Hahnamann matched most of Tommy's playing career," said Geoff. "He was great."

Jenna nodded. "He was."

"Since I'm a Christian, too, I always identified with Tommy because of his strong testimony. He wasn't ashamed to tell anyone what he believed. I remember reading articles in sports magazines as well as the Fellowship of Christian Athletes magazine where he talked openly about trusting Christ as his Savior."

Jenna stirred her tea. "He was very outspoken for the Lord."

"Then there was that Super Bowl game. I saw Tommy make that fabulous catch to win the game for Philadelphia. It was great!" Even now, more than four years later, Geoff's face took on the glow of the diehard sports fan.

"It was."

"You were married then?"

"Yes. We were married just after we graduated from Saunders College. Would you believe that I didn't even know who Tommy was when I transferred to Saunders for my junior year? He was already breaking records all over the place and attracting national media attention, but I'd never heard of him. I was too busy being a pianist. We met at Saunders' Christian Fellowship, and all I knew was that he was handsome and kind. I learned about famous later."

"Best pass receiver in college football history."

"So they said. Can I get you more coffee?"

After some casual conversation, Geoff left in more of Tommy's borrowed clothes, promising to return them. When he had gone, Jenna cleaned up the kitchen and scoured the bathroom. She made her bed and picked up the bedroom. But finally she could avoid it no longer. She opened the door to the guest room. She disliked working in here because Tommy was so ever-present.

She tugged at the sheets on the bed and threw them in a pile on the floor. As she did so, she saw herself doing this same chore over and over in the past, not with sheets merely wrinkled from use, but ones that were soiled and torn. The man who had slept here last night had slept soundly, not like Tommy had slept his last year tossing and turning in a sick, drunken stupor.

As she turned to pick up the sheets from the floor, she found herself looking into the picture of Tommy's last great catch, frozen forever in full color. She remembered her excitement as she had watched him run deep and leap for that ball. She had had no premonition as two men hit him on his way back to earth. How could she have known that while he had held onto the ball and won the Super Bowl, he had lost his career? How could she have known that the best of the best in the medical world wouldn't be able to make his knee whole again? How could she ever imagine that Tommy would be a has-been at twenty-five, a man who would walk with a permanent limp?

Waves of memory rushed over her as she stared at the picture. She had been so proud of Tommy as he put on a brave front, talking to reporters from his hospital bed and the rehabilitation center. But the off-season went by with no healing of the condition he hadn't really believed was permanent. Training camp and then pre-season began without him. When he heard the coach praise the wide receiver now playing his position as "another Tommy Mathisson," he had just gritted his teeth and smiled, though, in truth, the smile was getting thin.

Then came the Monday night when he watched the Eagles and never once heard anyone mention his name. That was the night the truth hit him.

From then on, Jenna had watched Tommy with growing concern. The faith that had been so vital to him when he was larger than life didn't seem to be mature enough now that he was mortal. He didn't seem able to accept that God could allow His servants to suffer—or that God's plans might be different from his.

"It's not fair, Jenn!"

The first time he screamed that sentence at her, she'd chalked it up to a hard day in therapy, nothing more. But as the frustration of the cry gave way to bitterness, Jenna tried to help him.

"Life's not fair, Tommy. Bad things happen to everyone at some time or another."

But Tommy's life had been so blessed that he couldn't handle the bad things. If you followed God, He blessed you. It was as simple as that to him. And to Tommy, blessings had been a professional football career and all the perks. Blessings couldn't be the silver lining in pain and loss of career.

"It's not fair" soon became "God's not fair." Although Tommy kept up all the proper Christian activities for some months, it was obvious to Jenna that there was a putrifying wound of bitterness beneath the neat skin of Tommy's faith. She feared the development of an open sore.

As he fought his spiritual battles, Tommy also fought

career ones. Jenna realized with a sinking heart that her husband was unprepared for anything but football.

"I'm going to be a TV sportscaster," he told her with great excitement one evening. "It's only a local station, but it's a step. Look at Tom Brookshire and Dick Vermeil and Jack Whitaker."

But the dream faded as Tommy had difficulty being the one asking the questions instead of the one being asked. And his growing bitterness showed with unexpected clarity on camera. At best, Tommy was merely adequate.

At the height of his playing career, companies had been falling all over themselves seeking Tommy's name for product endorsements.

"Now I've got some time, I'll do the endorsements," he told Jenna.

But now that he didn't have a career, no one wanted him.

He tried selling cars for a man who went to their church, but all Tommy did well with the customers was tell football stories.

Instead of trusting God in his despair, Tommy had allowed the well of bitterness to deepen. He began throwing money around to shore up his ego.

"Come out and see what I got," he shouted from the door of their luxurious, three-bedroom condominium one October evening. Jenna had gone out with him to find a beautiful silver BMW parked in the drive.

"Like it?" he asked proudly.

"It's a beautiful car," Jenna answered. "Whose is it?"

"Ours. I just bought it. Paid cash. Or I should say, it's yours. I'm going to get me a sports car."

She hugged him even as she eyed the car with

misgivings. The magnificent red Porsche he drove home two weeks later increased her apprehension. She found something unhealthy in his acquisition of things. He'd never needed them before.

One night as they prepared for bed, Jenna sighed.

"What's wrong, Jenn?" Tommy asked.

"Have you thought how our life has been divided in two by your injury? Things BK—before the knee—were so different from the way things are AK—after the knee."

"Are you complaining?" Tommy asked in a frosty voice that shriveled Jenna's heart. He obviously had heard personal attack where none was intended.

She hastened to his side. "Not at all, Tommy. I love you, not your knee or your football career or anything." She looked into his withdrawn face and tried to explain. "It's just that the injury seems to have changed your perspective on life so. It scares me sometimes. We don't have to be famous or rich to be happy. God will be faithful to us regardless of our circumstances."

"If God were faithful to us, our circumstances would never have changed," Tommy said, bitterness dripping.

"You mean you think that all faithful Christians should be rich? And have fine careers and healthy knees?"

He had simply stared at her coldly.

She shook her head. "That's not the way it is, Tommy. Look at the Apostle Paul and all the martyrs and the Christians in Communist bloc nations and in drought-stricken areas of Africa. Life isn't always the way we would script it. It's the way God wants it for reasons we can't even begin to fathom."

"Don't give me any more God stuff, Jenn. I can't handle

it. I feel too betrayed." And he had laid down with his back to her.

Hours later as she stared at the ceiling for yet another sleepless night, Jenna wondered how the human heart functioned, how she had come to the place of accepting God's sovereignty even though she couldn't understand it, and how Tommy had chosen to embrace bitterness instead.

Father—God—why doesn't he understand?

One morning in late November Tommy made another grandiose announcement. "I found us a great house," he had told Jenna. "We can move in by Christmas."

Jenna blanched at the thought of moving from the area where she was established—and just before Christmas yet. Mikey—Thomas Michael Mathisson, Jr.—would be almost three this Christmas, all entranced and enthralled. Jenna had looked forward to laughing with and at her small son, never quite admitting to herself that it would be therapy for the crying she did privately over his father.

Then, too, she wasn't feeling very well. She suspected she was pregnant.

"We can't possibly move that quickly," she said. "It'll take longer than that for the mortgage application to go through."

Tommy laughed and swung her around, a move she used to think was extremely romantic.

"The house is already paid for, Jenn. I gave the lady cash to expedite matters."

Jenna stared. "Cash? For a house?"

"A small place, don't worry. Only $200,000. Remember, we're rich. I earned over a million dollars for three years."

"But you don't see all that money, Tommy. You know that. Oughtn't we be careful until you're settled in a new job?"

His face fell into the harsh lines that darkened his face with increasing frequency. "Look, kitten, I bought the house. The deal is already closed. We're moving."

"But you never even asked me what I thought."

Tommy shrugged and left the house. When he had returned many hours later, Jenna smelled alcohol on his breath for the first time. It was that night that fear took up residence with the anxiety already in her heart.

6

The doorbell rang, and Jenna thankfully fled the room and its memories.

Stroking the rich green of the magnificent grape ivy the florist had just delivered, she read the card. "With many thanks! Geoff McGregor."

She had no trouble deciding where to hang Geoff's gift. The wandering Jew in front of the sliding glass door had long since wandered into its own barren wilderness and died. She placed the new plant on the hook Tommy had hung on one of his last good days and stood back to admire the effect.

"That's pretty, Mommy," said Libby. "It's big!"

Mikey was uninterested. He stood by the door with his bathing suit and towel in hand.

"Come on, Mom," he said. "I want to swim. The Tolys will be wondering where we are."

Acceding to her son's impatience, Jenna gave the lovely plant one last look as they walked out into the sweltering summer heat. As they climbed into the Ford Escort Jenna had gotten to replace the BMW, Libby said,

"Turn on the air conditioner, Mom." Her dark bangs were glued to her forehead.

Jenna turned the car key and listened to silence. She tried again and again, but the car refused to make even a burp. The battery? Did batteries die in the summer? In the TV ads, they always died in the winter.

She put up the hood and stood staring at the incomprehensible maze of her automobile's engine.

Lord, I can't afford a car repair bill. You know I really can't. And I certainly can't afford a towing bill.

"Are we going to be able to get to Tolys'?" called Mikey, hanging out the right front window of the car.

"I don't know."

Libby began to cry, her tears mixing with the sweat rolling down her face. "I want to go swimming. We never go swimming."

Since they had been to Tolys' twice last week to swim, Libby's sorrow didn't touch Jenna. The prospect of not having transportation for awhile was a totally different thing, though. Jenna felt herself panicking at the thought.

Suddenly a car braked to a stop in front of the house, backed up and pulled into the drive. Geoff McGregor climbed out.

"Having trouble?" he asked. "I saw the hood of the car up."

Jenna's woebegone eyes looked up at him as she pointed at the car.

"Can you fix it?" she asked cautiously, curiously.

Geoff looked at the engine, first from one angle, then another. He bent over and adjusted things, opened and closed things, pulled things out and thrust them back in again. He closed the hood and climbed into the driver's

46

seat. He got no more response than Jenna had.

"Can you fix it?" Jenna repeated without much hope.

He shook his head. "Nope. But it's easy to get fixed. Your only problem appears to be a dead battery. Have you got any jumper cables? I'll start your engine and follow you to a garage."

Jenna shook her head.

"Me neither," Geoff said. "We'll have to borrow some from a garage."

"We go to East Edge Eddie's," said Mikey who'd gotten out of the car to watch.

"How much does a battery cost?" Jenna asked. She dreaded the answer.

"Not much," said Geoff unhelpfully. He glanced at his watch. "Can you wait a couple of hours to get to the garage? I have an appointment with Dr. Rosell, my new boss, in fifteen minutes. When I'm finished, I can bring the cables back."

"Swimming, Mom," wailed Libby.

"Shh," said Jenna. Turning to Geoff, she said, "I have an appointment in fifteen minutes, too. And please tell me how expensive this whole thing will be."

Geoff looked at her, then at her beautiful house. She could almost hear him thinking, "Money troubles? Come on, now."

"Why don't I drop you where you're going and pick you up on my way home?" he suggested.

"We'll make you late."

"Not much. Where are you going?"

"I'm going downtown to The Lighthouse and the kids are going swimming at friends' who live on the way. And

47

be aware that I know you didn't answer my question."

Geoff laughed in surprise. "What's The Lighthouse? A restaurant? Or a mission?"

"Don't laugh. With me, money's serious stuff. And you're right. It's a mission. East Edge is just large enough to need one. The Lighthouse stands between two bars and across the street from the liquor store, right in the middle of the highest crime area in the county."

Geoff looked at Jenna curiously. "What do you do there? Tutor?"

"Teach piano. I have four students I meet every Friday afternoon. One's Trish Narducci; she and her husband Sal run the place. The others are three neighborhood ladies who've always wanted to play."

Just before the kids climbed out at the Tolys, Libby leaned over the seat and said, "Your plant's real pretty. Mommy hung it up."

"By the sliding door where we first met," said Jenna. "And I thank you. It's beautiful."

"My mother always told me that the way to a girl's heart was through flowers," Geoff said. "The years have proven her correct."

"A trail of broken hearts, huh?" Jenna looked at him. He was handsome in an understated way, tall, lean, with warm brown eyes and a strong, square jaw. His hair was dark, thick and straight except for a cowlick over his right temple that probably drove him crazy.

He looked at her and grinned. Had he felt her studying him? She turned away quickly, flustered. She grabbed for a safe topic of conversation.

"See that man over there?" Jenna pointed to a poorly dressed man shambling along the sidewalk with a paper bag hanging from each hand. On his feet were holey sneakers and no socks. His bony ankles hung out below pants too short in the inseam and too large in the waist. A rope served as a belt, and one end was draped over a shoulder like a solitary suspender and tied behind for security. His T-shirt, once white, was now a study in grays. His hair was raggedly cut and greasy, his beard unkempt.

"He showed up about a year ago and is frequently seen hiking around town, bags in hand."

Geoff studied the man in his rearview mirror. "Where does he sleep?"

"I have no idea. I've seen him out at the reservoir a couple of times, and I've seen him hiking the five miles into town. I know he hangs out at The Lighthouse looking for handouts. Sal's good with men like him. He talks with them and shares the gospel with them as well as feeds them."

"He looks like a New York or Philadelphia character, not one for a small city like East Edge."

Jenna agreed. "He fascinates my kids. They've never seen anyone like him. Mikey made up the name Charlie Wino for him."

"I bet he and Lt. Janczyn are acquainted," said Geoff.

Jenna nodded. "I would think so. How did your meeting with the lieutenant go this morning?"

"He's about as lovable in the morning as he is at night. But we got along fine. He's now convinced I'm reputable, thanks to Dr. Rosell. We went through the whole experience again and even went back out to the reservoir and walked the route I ran."

"Does he know anything or has he found any clues as to who was involved?"

"If he has, he didn't tell me. But he did suggest rather strongly that we not talk about what happened last night. There's a good chance those guys don't know who I am or where I went. If we can keep it that way, we greatly limit the already remote possibility that we might be in danger."

"*We* might be in danger?"

Geoff laughed. "Me. Not you. Don't worry. We're—I'm—completely anonymous to those men."

"You hope. *I* hope."

They stopped before The Lighthouse. Jenna collected her music and climbed out. "You're going to be late for Dr. Rosell."

"He's probably still at the hospital anyway."

"Make certain you tell him it's my fault."

Geoff just waved as he drove away. Jenna hurried into the storefront mission, almost stubbing her toe on the cinder block holding the door ajar. The long narrow room was fiercely hot and largely empty.

The smell of pine disinfectant was always the overriding sensory impression Jenna felt when she entered the place. Today's heat seemed to intensify the effect.

Near the front door, two cubicles roughly partitioned off gave a semblance of privacy for Sal and Trish in counseling situations. Two-thirds of the way back, a partition the width of the room separated the public area in front from the private. Behind this partition were the business office and two large closets that local churches tried to keep stocked with foodstuffs and clothes for The Lighthouse to distribute as needed.

In the public area, rows of chairs to accommodate fifty

were in place facing a rickety wooden pulpit. An old upright stood against the wall by the pulpit, and there waiting for Jenna was her first student, seventy-year-old Mrs. Washington.

Myrtle Washington had wanted to play the piano all her life. In fact, she had told Jenna the first day they met last September, "I have asked God for a chance to play the piano for as many years as I can remember. You are my answer to prayer."

The little black lady was squinting at the music of "The Old Rugged Cross." It was a fact that she needed glasses. It was also a fact that she refused to wear them.

"Mr. Washington didn't marry no girl with glasses. He's not goin' to have to live with one now."

Where Mrs. Washington had gotten her prejudice against glasses was anyone's guess, but after having met the bald, lensed, and dentured Mr. Washington, Jenna always laughed gently at the woman's needless vanity and enjoyed her indominatable spirit.

"Do your scales," Jenna said to the lady.

Mrs. Washington performed beautifully. You didn't need to see the music to do scales.

"Now a C chord."

Early on Mrs. Washington had discovered that if you began a chord in the lowest octave and rolled it repeatedly up the keyboard, it sounded like you knew what you were doing. Seventy-eight-year-old Mr. Washington was always properly impressed with her ability when she made him limp over to The Lighthouse and hear her. And you didn't need to see the music to roll the chords either.

When Mrs. Washington left, Thelma Smith took her place at the piano. Where Mrs. Washington made Jenna laugh, Thelma made her cry.

"I thought she'd never finish," Thelma said. She ran her fingers caressingly over the keys. Even her warm-ups were melodic, authoritative.

"Where are your kids today?" Jenna asked.

"My mom's got the two babies and my aunt's got Kareem. He loves to visit her. She lets him watch TV all the time. I only let him if he eats his food."

"Doesn't he eat well?" Three-year-old Kareem was eighteen-year-old Thelma's oldest child.

"Oh, he eats great." Thelma folded her hands over her rapidly expanding belly. "Keesha don't eat so well, but Keesha's a grump, not like Aneesha." Keesha and Aneesha were her year and a half old twins.

Kareem and the girls had the same father, a tall, gangly boy named Ray who used to escort Thelma to her lessons and wait for her to finish. Apparently he had nothing else to do with his time. But Ray had disappeared around February, and Jenna suspected the coming baby had been fathered by someone named Joby who figured more and more in Thelma's conversation.

"Have you ever thought of not having babies?" Jenna had asked once.

Thelma shrugged. "Yes and no. It's easier not to worry."

"But it's wrong to sleep with someone who's not your husband, Thelma. You know the Bible says that."

Thelma nodded. "Trish keeps telling me that. I keep telling her that it's just that everyone does it. There's nothing I can do."

"But what about your kids? What about you? Don't you want to do something with your life? Maybe go to school and study piano? Get off welfare?"

A brief gleam showed in Thelma's eyes. She blinked it away and said firmly, "Joby says he don't think education matters. You can do just fine without it."

The conversation had clearly closed.

Now Jenna listened with delight as Thelma played Beethoven's *Fur Elise*. If the girl didn't break a finger between now and tomorrow night, she should be the unexpected hit of the recital.

Jenna glanced at the clock on the wall.

"Oh, Thelma, we're way overtime. Poor Mrs. Coe."

Jenna looked around for her next student, but Mrs. Coe was nowhere in sight.

"Poor Mrs. Coe is right," said Thelma.

Jenna looked blank.

"That person what got killed and thrown in the reservoir last night—that was Bobby Coe, her son."

7

Jenna stared at Thelma aghast.

"The police came to Miz Coe's house this morning to tell her," Thelma said. "I heard her scream all the way to my house down the street."

Jenna felt sick at her stomach.

Trish Narducci walked through the partition door from the back of the room. Her usually smiling face was full of sorrow. "We've just come from the Coes'. Poor Addie."

Thelma nodded. "Poor Miz Coe."

Trish flopped onto one of the old folding chairs. "You don't mind if I don't take my lesson today, do you, Jenna? I just don't feel up to it."

"But you're still coming to the recital tomorrow night, aren't you?" asked Thelma quickly. She was the only one of The Lighthouse students performing, and pride and anxiety in equal parts filled her.

"Do you think Sal and I would miss your big moment? Don't worry; we'll be there."

"I got a new dress," said Thelma. "I don't even look pregnant in it."

Trish and Jenna looked at each other and smiled sadly at the girl's enthusiasm.

"Miz Coe loves her piano lessons," said Thelma apropos of nothing. "She's always telling me to appreciate what I got."

"Do they know who killed Bobby and why?" Jenna asked. The knowledge that she was now peripherally involved with the body in the reservoir on two fronts felt strange.

Trish shook her head. "They don't know anything yet, or if they do, they haven't told Addie."

"He knew too many things," said Thelma.

"Huh?" said Jenna.

"What?" asked Trish sharply.

Thelma shook her head, clearly regretting she had spoken. She grabbed her bag and sidled toward the door. "Just things," she said. "Too many things."

Jenna watched the girl as she stepped outside and made a wide arc around Charlie Wino leaning against the open door of the building.

"Is Thelma right, do you think?"

"I don't know," said Trish. "It's possible. It was an open secret that Bobby was into drugs. It caused Addie great grief. He'd served time at The Farms for dealing, and when he was released, there was no reason to think he'd quit. He had no visible job, yet he threw money around. It had to come from somewhere.

"But then he trusted Christ as his Savior two weeks ago."

"He did?" Jenna exclaimed in surprise. "That's wonderful!" *Maybe Bobby's life story didn't have a happy ending, but at least it wasn't a tragedy,* she thought.

Trish nodded. "Maybe he became a threat when he 'got religion' as he called it."

"Are drugs that prevalent in East Edge?"

Trish all but snorted. "Major industry, believe me, especially over the last year to year-and-a-half. At least around this area. There's unemployment, lack of education, lethargy, boredom, hopelessness—all the things that contribute to drugs. We can stand in the front window over there and watch a buy almost any hour of the day or night. Strung out addicts regularly come to us for help, but they only want our help until they can score again. That's why a genuine conversion like Bobby's was so special."

Trish stood up and began pacing aimlessly.

"Bobby was a great dodger," she said. "He kept blaming everybody else for his troubles—his father because he ran out on the family, the schools because they didn't make him a scholar, the 'system' for not getting him a good paying job, the disadvantage of his blackness, or anything else he could think of. Sal kept holding him accountable for his own wrong choices. Then, finally, Bobby could say, 'God, be merciful to me, a sinner'."

"How old was Bobby?"

"Twenty-five. He was Addie's baby. Mr. Coe was a loser who went to the bar one evening twenty years ago and never came home. No one knows what became of him. Eddie's the oldest son. He's in Graterford Prison for murder. There's a daughter, Miranda, a beauty judging by her pictures. She ran away about eight years ago to make her fortune as a model and actually succeeded. But she wants nothing to do with her family. Addie keeps track of her through her advertisements. Addie came running in here last week because she saw Miranda in an aspirin ad on TV. She was so proud, but it was sad."

"I never knew Addie's life was so hard," said Jenna, feeling very unperceptive. "When she talked with me, she was always so positive. She always tried to encourage me because she knew I was a widow."

Trish nodded. "I think Addie chooses every day not to be bitter. She's a great lady."

Sal Narducci walked in the front door carrying a sweating six pack of soft drinks.

"I knew if I bought some extras, there'd be someone to drink them with us," he said.

The three moved to the business office and Sal propped his feet on his desk. In the corner an old fan chugged in a valiant, though largely vain, effort to move the sticky air.

"Some days I don't feel up to this ministry," he said as he snapped a tab and took a long drink of the cold soda. "I must be getting old."

Jenna grinned. Sal was about her age.

"And the hardest part," he continued, "is that there's so little I can do to ease the problems because they are so complicated. Someone like Bobby becomes a Christian and it's wonderful and it's great and I rejoice. All the spiritual consequences in his life change because of Christ's forgiveness. But his life is still as complicated as it ever was."

"Don't take the whole burden on yourself, Sal," Trish said. "You know better."

He nodded. "I do. But I'd still give my eyeteeth to have some place to send people like Bobby so they can become grounded in the Lord, ordered in their private lives, and be away from danger and temptation for awhile. Though," he said as a sadness crept into his voice, "I know that sometimes, even with the best intentions, things can't be straightened out."

"Sal," said Trish. She reached across the desk and put her hand on her husband's. "Don't."

"Did you know I had a younger brother, Jenna?" asked Sal, turning his hand over to squeeze Trish's.

Jenna shook her head.

"Nick. Two years younger. We were a team as kids, him and me. Our father was an alcoholic and our mother only remembered to come home every so often. Childhood for me was the pits. The only good memory I have is laughing with Nick over some of our escapades.

"We thought we'd really struck gold when we stumbled onto the big money involved in dealing drugs. By the time we were in our late teens and early twenties, we were rich. We had so much money that we took to burying it in the back yard in old mayonnaise jars. We had motorcycles, flashy clothes, girls, everything we thought we wanted. We also had roaring cases of paranoia and were physical wrecks.

"Then I got arrested for possessing and selling drugs and was sent to The Farms. It was there that I heard about Christ and accepted Him as my Savior. I couldn't wait to tell Nick so he could find the same new—and joyful—life I had found.

"But Nick wasn't interested. He liked his life the way it was. He especially liked the drugs. I was a senior in Bible school the year he died of an overdose in a flophouse in Philadelphia."

Jenna had heard about the mayonnaise jars, the

material abundance, and the spiritual poverty before. But this was the first time she'd heard about Nick.

"The thing that never quite leaves me is that I'm the one who turned Nick on to drugs. Even though I became a believer and my spiritual slate was wiped clean, the practical consequences of my life before Christ continued."

A somber silence held the three until Sal broke it by tossing his now empty soda can at the wastebasket and missing. He got up and put it in the basket.

"Sorry. I don't usually get so maudlin. It's Bobby that makes me feel this way, I guess."

"Don't apologize. I feel awful and I didn't even know him, only his mother," said Jenna.

"Excuse me, Sal." A tall man with slightly greying brown hair stood apologetically at the office door. "Harley and I have a load of things in my car for the food closet."

Sal bounded to his feet, his sorrow pushed aside for the moment.

"Wonderful, Rolf! Let's bring the stuff in."

"Hi, Jenna," said Rolf Wyland. "What are you doing here?"

"I give piano lessons here every Friday afternoon."

"You have a busy Friday." Rolf's daughter Valerie was one of Jenna's Friday after school students. "I also hear you had a busy night out your way last night."

For some reason Jenna was reluctant to talk about Bobby, and she certainly wasn't going to spread the news of Geoff's and her involvement. She just nodded and said, "From what I understand, the body was found some distance from my house."

Rolf nodded. "Just don't you go wandering around out

there at night. I don't want to have to find another piano teacher for Valerie. I'm sure there's none as pleasing to look at within miles."

Jenna smiled politely at the heavy-handed compliment.

"Hey, Mrs. Mathisson," said Harley Tester as Jenna walked back to the alley to help Sal, Trish and Rolf carry in great quantities of foodstuffs. "How are you doing? I haven't seen you in a long time."

"That must be because your boss—" She looked at Rolf with a smile, "—is keeping you so busy that you haven't even time to fish anymore. Mikey misses 'helping' you at the bridge."

Harley laughed, pleased to be missed. He was a strong, sturdy man with a head of glorious red curls. However it wasn't his looks that set him apart; it was his height. Harley was a little person, and one of the reasons Mikey liked to fish with him was because Harley was close to his eye level.

"I've been awfully busy. You knew I've been helping Rolf coach his son's Little League team, didn't you?" said Harley.

"No, I didn't," Jenna answered as she filled a paper bag with cans. "Is your team any good?"

"As a team we're acceptable and that's about it, but we have a couple of good players. Rolf's son Sean is one of them. When the season's over, maybe I'll have some time to fish."

Jenna flipped open a box and began filling it for Sal to carry. "And how's business? Does Little League leave time for the gas station?"

"Things at the station are real busy," Harley said happily. "Since we put in that pair of diesel pumps, we get

61

a lot more traffic from the bypass. It's not unusual to see four, five rigs there at a time. Now we need a place where the truckers can sit and relax, play a video game or two, get a bite to eat."

"A full scale truck stop? You guys *are* doing well."

"We'd do better if the boss came to work long enough to see what we need," said Harley to Rolf's back as the man walked into the mission with his arms full of boxes of canned goods.

"Yeah, yeah, yeah," Rolf called good-naturedly over his shoulder.

Harley grinned. "The man's an idiot and a genius. He's an idiot because he's letting great potential go untapped at the station. But he's a genius because he's spending all the time he's not at the garage studying and playing the stock market. It began as a hobby and now it's an obsession. I tell you, if his ex-wife ever found out how much he's really worth, she'd have him back in court in an instant."

"And she'd better never find out," pronounced Rolf as he returned to collect another load.

Grinning, Harley handed Rolf the heaviest box remaining. He gave Jenna five loaves of bread.

When the trunk was empty, Rolf and Harley waved good-bye and were gone.

"Interesting man," said Sal. "Rolf comes once or twice a month with great gobs of food, and I don't even think he's a Christian. Just altruistic."

"Where does he get the food?" asked Jenna. "He doesn't buy it all himself, does he?"

Sal shook his head. "They have a collection bin at the gas station right next to the pumps. Whenever it gets full, they bring the stuff here. They also turn in contributions from the truckers."

"People are so surprising," said Trish. "They hardly ever do what you'd expect."

Charlie Wino shuffled into the front room of The Lighthouse, bags in hand.

"And here we have one of the most interesting," said Sal, not unkindly. "I don't know how many times I've talked to the man and after each conversation I realize I've learned nothing about him. I don't even know his real name. He answers to whatever you call him. We usually just call him Charlie. He's a master at the verbal dodge."

"He fascinates Mikey," said Jenna. "He calls him Charlie Wino."

Sal laughed. "I love it." He walked to the derelict. "What can I do for you, Charlie?"

"I've got to go," Jenna said, gathering her books. "I've got lessons to give at home in a little while."

"Okay," said Trish. "We'll see you tomorrow night. How about going out for some ice cream after the big performance?"

"The kids will have to be with me," said Jenna.

"No problem," said Trish, turning to leave. "I've got to go hear Charlie's latest story. He has the most creative lines of anyone who comes in here."

Jenna was at the front door when she remembered she couldn't go anywhere. Realizing it might be several minutes before Geoff came, she sat down in a chair inside the front door and waited. As she did, she studied Charlie Wino.

He always made her somewhat uneasy. He reminded

her of the bums she used to see as a little girl when her father would drive the family to Philadelphia from their home in New Jersey. Just at the Pennsylvania side of the Ben Franklin Bridge was a park that was always full of shaggy, loafing men. She and her brothers had called the park Bum Park, and it was always a wonder to them that men would live that way.

Charlie Wino should have lived in Bum Park. Then he could have hung around the old Sunday Breakfast Mission. Since he lived in East Edge instead, he hung around The Lighthouse begging, drinking, whining about injustices. No one knew where he came from.

The thing about Charlie that made Jenna uncomfortable were the flashes of intelligence that he couldn't quite hide. He tried to keep his eyes vacant, his face devoid of emotion. But there was a keen mind under that unkempt hair, and try as he would to hide it, it showed. Charlie Wino was a man who didn't need to lug his world about in two bags. Why did he?

Jenna watched the Narduccis deal with Charlie with something like awe. Trish was five feet and weighed a hundred pounds, but nothing seemed to faze her. Smelly men like Charlie Wino were all in a day's work. She had as strong a burden for the people their mission touched as Sal did, and she complemented him well. Where Sal was a big, outspoken man, a product of the streets and an ex-con, Trish was from a stable Christian family and blessed with enormous tact and a boundless sense of humor. The two had met in Bible school and come to East Edge three years ago to establish The Lighthouse. It had been a hard and demanding three years and Jenna knew money—or rather the lack of money—was always a problem.

"Charlie, you know better than that," said Sal somewhat sharply.

"How do I know better than that?" the man snapped back. "I'm just looking to score. Bobby was my source. If I could find out where he got it, then I'd be okay. He came to see you a lot. Maybe he got it here." The man looked slyly at Sal. "You're a junkie."

"An ex-junkie, Charlie. Big difference. And you know very well Bobby didn't get any drugs here."

Charlie nodded, skeptically. "I hear you talking." Obviously he was far from convinced.

Sal was about to respond when Trish laid her hand on his arm. He looked at her and she shook her head ever so slightly. Sal closed his mouth. She was right; argument was fruitless.

"Charlie," Trish said, "have you had anything to eat today?"

Charlie thought for a moment. "I don't think so."

"Come on, then. Let's get you a cup of coffee and a bowl of cereal."

"No ham and eggs?"

"No ham and eggs. No stove to cook them on."

Charlie frowned, then shrugged. "Hey, who am I to complain? Free is free. How about if I sing for my supper?"

Sal, Trish and Charlie walked through the partition to the back of the mission while Charlie sang "Jesus Loves Me" at the top of his lungs. Without missing a beat he turned sideways so he and his bags could slip neatly through the doorway.

At the last minute Trish turned around, looked at Jenna, and gave a big wink.

8

Finally Geoff arrived.

"I'm sorry I'm so late," he said as he came inside the mission. "Dr. Rosell was delayed at the hospital just like we said might happen. Have I thrown your schedule completely out of whack?"

Jenna hesitated. "No. But can I ask a favor?"

"Sure."

"One of my students is the mother of the man who was thrown in the reservoir last night."

Geoff whistled softly. "Did you know the victim, too?"

Jenna shook her head. "But I'd like to go visit Mrs. Coe. Just for a few minutes."

Geoff looked at her assessingly. "You sure? It'll be pretty emotional over there."

"I know. That's why I'd like to go see her. I remember how much people's presence helped me. Gus Glassman, the Eagles' coach, drove out personally to see me. I remember how grateful I was to him because I knew he didn't have to do that."

"And you're Mrs. Coe's Gus Glassman."

She searched his face for mockery but found only understanding. "Yes, you could put it that way."

Geoff got directions from Trish, observed hostilely by Charlie Wino because he had interrupted their conversation, and easily found North Street. It was lined with old row homes that had seen better days. Many were afflicted with sagging steps and leaning porches, and Mrs. Coe's place needed paint badly. But her front patch of yard was aglow with brave zinnias and marigolds. Healthy philodendrons and wandering Jews hung from her porch roof.

Jenna's heart beat too fast, and her stomach felt cramped as she approached the door. She was grateful for Geoff's presence.

A large black woman answered the knock at the door. She was openly unhappy at the sight of Jenna and Geoff.

"I'm Jenna Mathisson, Mrs. Coe's piano teacher. She usually sees me Friday afternoons for lessons at The Lighthouse."

"I know about the lessons," said the woman as she folded her arms across her ample bosom. She filled the entire doorway with her bulk. She was obviously unimpressed by Jenna's status.

Jenna pressed on. "I just learned about Bobby a little bit ago." She swallowed. This woman, whoever she was, was a powerful protector. She certainly scared Jenna. "May I see Mrs. Coe for a few moments?"

"Why?"

Why. Jenna said the first thing that came to mind. "Because I'm a widow and I know what it's like to hurt."

The woman stared at Jenna, then shifted her gaze to Geoff.

"Who's he?"

"A friend. He drove me here because my car's broken."

"He's not a reporter?"

Suddenly Jenna understood the woman's caution. "No, he's not a reporter. He's a doctor."

The woman raised her eyebrows at this last piece of information and scrutinized Geoff openly.

"He don't look like no doctor to me. He's too young."

Jenna looked quickly at the porch floor to hide her smile while Geoff cleared his throat self-consciously.

The woman looked closely at them again, then stepped aside and invited them in.

"I'm Addie's sister, Louise," she said. "I just don't want Addie gettin' hurt no more."

"I don't blame you for being cautious," said Jenna. "Mrs. Coe's fortunate to have someone who cares so much."

Louise led them through the house to the kitchen. The living room and dining room furniture was old, but the place was neat and clean. A framed picture of a young man in a cap and gown sat on a large TV. A stack of library books sat on an end table. The walls were decorated with Christian posters and some poorly stretched needlework.

Green plants sat on almost every available spot. One of the biggest jade plants Jenna had ever seen filled the dining room window. The kitchen was bright with afternoon sunlight and four geraniums reposed on the windowsill over the sink, rejuvenating themselves after their winter's rest.

Addie Coe sat at the kitchen table with an untouched glass of iced tea in front of her. A small bottle of uncapped tranquilizers sat on the table, and one small pill lay beside the iced tea. Addie appeared to be studying it. She stood up in surprise when she saw Jenna and Geoff.

"Oh," was all she could say.

"Mrs. Coe, I'm so sorry," Jenna said.

The two women met mid-kitchen and clasped hands tightly. Geoff stepped into the background as Louise began to cry. Obviously her formidable appearance masked a deeply sorrowing heart.

"Ah, Jenna." Mrs. Coe's face was seamed with pain. "These men have no idea the hurt that they bring, do they?"

Jenna's eyes filled. "No," she whispered. "They don't."

The two women hugged each other silently, members of the sorority of shared pain.

Mrs. Coe pulled back and began to talk.

"They identified Bobby by his high school ring, Jenna. He'd been beat up too bad to be recognized."

Louise shook her head at the awfulness of it all and reached for a new tissue.

"He was the first one in our family to graduate from high school, you know?" Addie said. "Mr. Coe and me didn't have no chance to finish. We both had to go to work when we was real young.

"Eddie never finished school even though I kept telling

70

him and telling him to." She sighed. "He wasn't dumb. He could have done it. But he never listened about nothing, that boy. School was just one more thing he knew better than me about."

Addie looked at a bulletin board hanging on the wall behind the table. It was filled with four color ads cut out of magazines, all featuring a beautiful black woman smiling warmly at the camera.

"And that Miranda, she ran away before she got done tenth grade. Just disappeared one day when she was sixteen. No warning, no notes, no nothing. Just gone, like her daddy. We didn't know where she was for a long time. Then I got a postcard from New York City. She said she was all right, and I guess she is. But every time I see the pictures of them missing kids at the post office or on the milk cartons, I know what their mamas is feeling." Addie nodded. "I know."

She wrapped her arms around herself as if trying to keep warm. The temperature was in the high eighties.

"But Bobby, he finished school. I was so proud. When I went to that graduation and they called out Robert James Coe, I cried."

She wiped at her eyes, nodding to herself at the memory.

"He was proud, too. He never said nothing, but he saved his money 'til he could get that ring. He was just a kid, but he saved his money. It had a ruby in it, all pretty and red, and it said 1984 on it and it had his initials inside."

Mrs. Coe began to cry, her face twisting in pain. "They said they'll give it back to me later."

"Come on, Addie." Louise wiped her own tears and put her arm around her sister's shoulders, leading her back to the table. Addie collapsed in her chair and sobbed into her hands.

"I'm sorry," she wheezed, ashamed.

"Don't be. It's good." Jenna leaned over and kissed the woman's wet cheek. "I just wanted you to know that I cared and that I'll be praying for you."

Touching the woman lightly on the shoulder, Jenna turned to Geoff and silently they let themselves out. Geoff took Jenna's elbow to help her down the rickety stairs and kept it there as they walked to the car. She was grateful to him. Unshed tears blurred her vision.

"Hey, Miz Mathisson!" a bright voice called. "How is she?"

Jenna looked at Thelma, all energy and vitality, pushing a double stroller down the street. A tall, incredibly handsome young black man trailed behind her as she pushed the stroller up to Jenna.

"Is she okay?" Thelma asked again. "She's a real nice lady."

"She'll be all right," Jenna said. "Right now she's just heartbroken."

Thelma nodded, trying to imagine what it was like to be Mrs. Coe and failing. She shrugged and pushed the stroller until it all but touched Jenna's shins.

"This is Keesha and Aneesha," she said proudly.

Jenna looked at the little girls, their hair caught up in tiny braided pigtails all over their heads. They were adorable, but Jenna could see what Thelma meant about Keesha being a grump. Her baby face scowled while Aneesha beamed happily around her thumb.

Jenna knelt and oohed and aahed at the little girls. Even Geoff made appropriate noises.

Thelma grabbed her escort by the arm. "This is my piano teacher," she told him excitedly, pointing at Jenna.

The young man looked at both Jenna and Geoff with unconcealed hostility, not acknowledging the introduction. While his displeasure seemed a bit extreme, Jenna thought she understood. She and this young man were truly rivals for Thelma's attentions. Jenna prayed she won.

"She's in charge where I'm playing tomorrow night," said Thelma happily. "I told you I got a new dress, didn't I, Miz Mathisson? Did I tell you my grandmom's coming? She's bringing Kareem."

Jenna doubted that three-year-old Kareem would be that impressed by his mother's playing. In fact, she doubted that the child would be anything but bored. But at least Thelma would have some family support for her performance and that was encouraging.

Thelma pulled the man with her forward.

"This is Joby White." It was an announcement.

Jenna wasn't certain of the etiquette of such situations, so she stuck out her hand. Joby shook it gracelessly, remaining silent, cold.

Jenna made her introduction. "This is Dr. McGregor."

Thelma stared at Geoff, surprised. "Does Miz Coe need a doctor?"

"N-no," Jenna stammered. How did she explain Geoff without Thelma jumping to wrong and romantic conclusions? "He's not here because of her. I mean, of course he's here because of her but he's not here *for* her. I mean . . . well . . . ."

Thelma and Joby looked at Jenna quizzically.

Geoff spoke. "Mrs. Coe is doing as well as can be expected." Then he took Jenna's elbow again and pushed her into the car.

Jenna fought the impulse to giggle as they drove away. " 'As well as can be expected'! 'As well as can be expected'!"

Geoff grinned at her. "It sure beats, 'N-no . . . I mean . . . I mean . . . well . . . .' "

She giggled. "It does."

Her eye caught sight of the clock on the dash.

"Geoff! It's 3:50! I've got to get home! I've got a student coming at 4:00!"

9

Geoff took the shorter back road out of East Edge. It followed Stony Creek as it wound its way to the reservoir. At one point the land on the right fell off abruptly, and Stony Creek became only a silver band on the floor of a small, narrow valley.

"The original reservoir was located here many, many years ago," said Jenna. "These small homes perched on the side of the hill used to be boat houses that opened onto the water."

Geoff glanced with interest at the area. It was easy to picture the valley filled with water, dotted with rowboats and canoes holding ladies with silk parasols and gentlemen in straw hats.

"I guess they built the new reservoir because they needed a bigger one?"

"I don't know," said Jenna. "Maybe the dam became unsafe. Maybe it was too close to East Edge." She shrugged.

Driving as swiftly as was safe, they passed the last house, and the edge of the drop-off became overrun with weeds and small bushes that grew out onto the road, narrowing it appreciably.

Suddenly there was a great *thud* and the car veered wildly. Geoff muttered under his breath as he wrestled with the wheel, struggling to hold the car on the road.

"What's wrong?" Jenna exclaimed even as the car lurched sharply a second time, throwing her forward. She was stopped abruptly by her seat belt just before she hit the dash and the window. The car shuddered as if in pain.

Geoff gripped the wheel and glanced in his rearview mirror.

"There's a mad man behind us who's ramming us!" he shouted.

Jenna swung around and watched in horror as a white car, inches from their rear bumper, swung out into the left lane and drew up beside them. She knew exactly what the driver was going to do.

"Watch it, Geoff!" she screamed.

Before the words were even out of her mouth, they were struck heavily at the front left fender as the white car turned deliberately, destructively into them. The grinding noise of metal rasping against metal was terrible to hear.

Geoff wrestled desperately with the wheel as they brushed against the white wooden pilings that lined the small cliff. Jenna knew with terrible certainty that the little pilings with steel cable stretched between would never hold them on the road if the white car forced their car fully into them.

Jenna stared with stunned fascination at the vehicle beside them. The driver turned and seemed to look directly at her. He was wearing a ski mask and a jacket, a violent and anonymous destroyer.

Pulling her eyes away from the person, Jenna realized sickly that they had been forced to the very edge of the road. One more hard hit and they would go over. The thought of the tumbling fall to the unforgiving floor of the valley made her tremble, and she fought her heaving stomach.

Suddenly, desperately scanning the road, she pointed a shaking hand to a small break in the white pilings.

"Driveway!" she screamed.

"Driveway!" Geoff screamed back as he hit the brakes and wrenched the wheel to the right.

Jenna braced herself as they shot off the road onto a steep, gravel roadbed that led to the floor of the valley and a lone log house built there long ago by a disgruntled nonconformist. The tires slewed from side to side as Geoff struggled to hold the car on the narrow, slippery drive. At one point Jenna was certain the front wheel on her side left the roadbed and hung in midair.

Finally, long seconds later, in a flurry of gravel they came to a shuddering halt on the valley floor at the edge of the abandoned cabin's yard.

Dust motes dancing gracefully in the sunlight and the tranquil calm of Stony Creek flowing a few feet away contrasted dramatically with Jenna's terror as she glanced fearfully behind her, half expecting the menacing car to have followed them down the drive. But there was nothing to see except a frightened dog.

Geoff and Jenna stared at each other as the silence buffeted their ears.

"Are you okay?" he asked at last.

Unable to speak, Jenna nodded.

Geoff leaned forward and dropped his head on the

steering wheel, shoulders slumped.

"Are you all right?" Jenna asked around the cottony feeling in her mouth. She leaned toward him, concerned, laying a hand on his arm. He'd had such a rough time last night and now this.

He straightened with deliberate effort. "Fine."

She looked at him doubtfully.

He grinned wearily. "Well, when the alternative is being crunched at the bottom of the ravine, I'm great."

She couldn't help but smile back, and some of the tension drained away.

"Did you happen to notice what kind of car it was?" Geoff asked.

"No. Everything was so unbelievable, and I'm no good at cars. It was just a white car. Don't you know what it was?"

"No." His hands clenched on the wheel. "I was a bit preoccupied."

She nodded. "Did he follow us from town?"

"I don't know. All of a sudden he was just there."

She leaned her head wearily on the back of the seat and watched a Monarch butterfly cavort in the sunshine.

"And was it a he?" Geoff asked.

"I don't know." She rubbed her arms as she shivered in the summer heat. "He wore a ski mask and a jacket."

Geoff nodded. "Can't say I'm surprised. I just want to know how he knew who we were and where to find us."

"Do you think this was connected with last night?" Jenna said.

"Don't you think it has to be?"

Reluctantly, fearfully, Jenna met Geoff's somber gaze

and nodded slightly. The eerie, prickling sensation from the night before crept up her spine again. "Someone knows who you are and where you escaped to, don't they?" Jenna asked softly.

Geoff's dark, silent expression answered her. Gripping her hands tightly together, Jenna tried to accept the fact that somehow she had become a murderer's quarry.

When their car stuck its nose out of the drive, Jenna looked fearfully to the right and left. She half expected their attacker to be lying in wait for them though reason told her he would be gone. All the way home, she kept looking over her shoulder, but the white car never reappeared.

When they got to her house, Jenna was startled to find Alex and his mother waiting in the drive. She had forgotten all about her piano students. She was almost half an hour late.

"Tell them to go," said Geoff.

Jenna shook her head. "I can't. First, I need the money. Secondly, tomorrow night's the recital and I need to see him and then Valerie to be certain they're ready."

He nodded. "Okay. I'll call Lt. Janczyn from my place and then I'll get Mikey and Libby and the jumper cables for you."

She looked at him gratefully. "Thank you."

Jenna walked to her door and unlocked it, proud that her hand barely shook. Already the attack seemed far away, more imagination than reality. But the soreness in her chest from being slammed against the seat belt was grim proof that the incident had indeed occurred.

"I know my pieces really well," Alex said proudly as he sat down at the piano. Jenna forced herself to concentrate as he played Edna May Burnam's *Mechanical Man* and *Summer Rain* flawlessly, if quickly.

"For not liking piano, I do really good, don't I?" Alex grinned precociously.

The doorbell rang halfway into Alex's second run-through, and Valerie Wyland let herself in. She quietly took a seat until Alex and Jenna finished. Her long blonde braid hung down her back, and her white sandaled feet were primly crossed as she waited her turn.

Jenna had often wondered how her parents' divorce had affected Valerie. She was a quiet, intense thirteen-year-old, the kind who feels deeply but often can't express or explain what she is thinking. She was just the opposite of Alex, who probably had never had a reflective thought in his whole short life.

Jenna knew she had thought more about Valerie than necessary because it was obvious that Rolf would like his and Jenna's friendship to be more than casual. While Jenna had no such wish, she had wondered many times how Valerie would respond to a stepmother. She didn't think the child would do well.

Valerie's lesson went quickly. She was definitely prepared for the recital as she carefully and ably played Bach's *Minuet In G*.

Jenna listened sadly. It was a tragedy of sorts that the girl made no emotional connection with her music. Admittedly she was only thirteen. Maybe with maturity she would be able to make her music talk, but Jenna doubted it. It was just Valerie's flaw to have fine technique and lack that indefinable spark. Still, Valerie was a pleasant child and Jenna enjoyed teaching her.

Geoff and the kids arrived at the same time Rolf Wyland

came to pick up Valerie for their usual weekend together. Alex was still waiting for his mom.

Everyone congregated at the front door and Jenna introduced Geoff to Rolf and Valerie. She was amused at the once over Rolf gave Geoff.

"So you're going to be Ben Rosell's new associate," Rolf said as the men shook hands. "Ben was talking about you just last week when we played golf. He's looking forward to having you join him."

"That's nice to hear." Geoff looked pleased.

"Do you golf?" Rolf asked. It was clear by his inflection that Geoff's answer would establish his place forever in the man's personal estimation.

Geoff, aware, grinned. "I play at it. I enjoy golf a lot, but these past few years, I haven't had much time to work on my game. My brother-in-law, Arch Steager, left me his clubs while he's on vacation, and I mean to use them before he comes home."

"How about tomorrow morning?" Rolf asked. "The good Dr. Rosell can't come tomorrow because of some wedding or something."

"Rolf, his son's getting married, and you know it," Jenna chided.

Rolf was unrepentant. "Anything that interferes with a game of golf is foolish."

Valerie blinked and studied her feet to hide a frown.

"I'd like to join you, Rolf," said Geoff. "What time?"

"Seven-thirty. I'll meet you on the practice green."

Rolf put his hand on Valerie's shoulder and pretended not to notice when she stepped back from his touch. He carelessly slid both hands in his pants pockets.

"Come on, Val, my love. Quick dinner, then off to Sean's

game." He turned to Geoff and tried to be casual as he said, "My son plays on the Little League All-Star team, and tonight's their first game."

As Rolf and Valerie disappeared from view, Alex's mother finally returned for her son. The woman was Jenna's thorn in the side. She seemed to view piano teachers somewhere toward the bottom in life's pecking order. She never minded missing lessons, being late bringing Alex, picking him up, or "forgetting" to pay. She'd once called Jenna a cheap money grubber because Jenna had asked for two months back payments.

"What time tomorrow night?" she called shrilly from her car. "I don't know how to make our plans."

Jenna, who three weeks ago had sent home a paper with all the pertinent information, answered evenly, "Try to be there by 6:45. The program begins at 7:00."

"At Calvary Church?"

"At Calvary Church, just like the last two years."

"Do I detect a slight note of asperity in your voice?" asked Geoff as they watched Alex and his mother drive away.

"That woman drives me crazy. You'd think I was in business for her convenience only, not my financial well-being." She sighed, then dismissed Alex's mother from her mind as not worth the emotional drain. "How'd it go with Lt. Janczyn and when do I get my car fixed?"

"The Lieutenant and I had a nice talk, and he wants a list of everyone we both talked to today."

"Everyone?"

Geoff said, in an exaggerated imitation of Lt. Janczyn, " 'Everyone, Dr. McGregor. I don't care how unlikely a suspect he or she seems. Everyone.' " He frowned just like

82

Lt. Janczyn, and Jenna couldn't help grinning. "And Eddie said he'd work on your car tomorrow afternoon."

"Not until then?"

"He says he's busy, and it's the best he can do. He says you've got to understand. But he did give me the cables. I'll stop down about noon tomorrow, and we'll jump start your car. I can follow you in to East Edge to make certain you get there all right."

"I appreciate your help immensely, Geoff. I know I must be putting you out and interfering with your vacation, and I do thank you."

"Look, you rescued me last night and saved both our necks this afternoon. Now I rescue you. Just call it a mutual assistance society."

He smiled at her, and suddenly she could barely breathe. The very air seemed to pulse with emotion. It was a crystal moment, forever frozen, yet fluid with unexpected possibilities. And she could see that Geoff felt it, too. An expression of surprise flashed across his face as he looked at her.

"Mom!" Libby grabbed Jenna about the legs, and the fragile moment shattered. "I'm hungry!"

"Me, too," Mikey announced, coming up behind his sister.

"Well," said Jenna, searching for her breath and her ability to reason, "I'm sure I can find us something if you just give me some time." She patted Libby's hair absently, trying to understand what had just happened, trying to decide if she had imagined it.

"I guess I'd better go," said Geoff, his feet planted firmly on Jenna's walk.

Jenna nodded, desperately wanting him to stay, still too

bemused to speak.

"Why don't you eat with us?" asked Libby graciously. "We like to have company. Don't we, Mommy? We can have something very special like hot dogs, if you'd like."

Geoff grinned. "Thank you. I'd like that. That is, if your mother says it's all right."

Still tongue-tied, but grateful for her daughter's artless hospitality, Jenna nodded and led the way inside.

Dinner was hot dogs at Libby's insistence. It was also potato salad, baked beans, tossed salad and laughter as Geoff told the kids his favorite jokes collected from his small patients.

After dinner Geoff planted himself at the sink, rinsed the dishes, and loaded the dishwasher.

Jenna watched until she could stand it no longer.

"When you get married, do you plan to be a model husband and do the dishes for your wife?"

"Not if I have anything to say about it," Geoff said.

Jenna shrugged mentally, while she smiled at his teasing tone. One couldn't really expect perfection.

Geoff continued, "I hate doing the dishes. It's a sign of my esteem for women who take in bleeding strangers and magically create hidden driveways that I'm standing here right now. Besides, I don't know where to put things away, and I can't just stand and stare while you do all the work. Can you get away for a few hours?"

Jenna, who had been putting leftover potato salad in the refrigerator, swung around sharply at his last sentence.

With regret she shook her head. "I've no one to leave the kids with."

"Tomorrow night? Dinner?"

"My recital."

"Afterward?"

"There're still the kids. The Tolys had them today and will again tomorrow afternoon so I can be certain everything's arranged for the recital. I can't ask them for tomorrow night too. Janie and Arch, my favorite babysitters, are away. Besides, I'm supposed to go out with the Narduccis for ice cream after the recital. The kids, too."

"No way to rearrange? Let the Narduccis take just the kids?"

"I'll see what I can do."

"Is it always so hard to get free?"

Jenna nodded. "Believe it or not, going out for ice cream tomorrow night is a big thing. Tight finances make babysitters a rare treat, and friends can only be taken advantage of so often. The only thing I do with any regularity besides go to church is sing with the Chester County Christian Chorale. Janie keeps the kids for me every Tuesday night so I can do that."

Geoff looked at her closely. "It's been hard." It was a statement.

She closed her eyes as she agreed. "It's been hard."

"I don't understand why. I don't mean the grief. I mean the finances. Tommy made a fortune. Even I know that."

Jenna shrugged. "It's not too difficult, really. It's just ugly. Tommy went sort of crazy before he died. He began drinking to drown his bitterness over his knee. Then he started betting, first on sporting events, then at Atlantic City. And I don't mean the slot machines, either. He also became a conspicuous consumer. When he finally drove his red Porsche into a tree, he had so many debts that everything went to pay them off, even the insurance money."

Jenna looked around the comfortable family room in which they now sat.

"When Tommy first died, I wanted to stay in this house for the kids' sakes—and mine. It was our link with the past. It was continuity. It was a known in a world gone crazy.

"Recently I've begun to wonder, though, if perhaps the house doesn't hold me hostage to the past. Perhaps it's time for us to move to another place where we can be the three of us, not echoes of Tommy."

"Certainly it would ease your financial situation," Geoff said practically.

"You sound just like Arch. He's been advising me to sell for a long time. But it's not so much a matter of logic as it is of emotion. For a long time I simply didn't have the emotional strength to go through the trauma of a move. I was so spent from trying to live each day that I had nothing left over for something as overwhelming and threatening as a move. Every time someone suggested it, I felt a wave of panic wash over me. Besides, I love this house and its location. I hate to give it up."

She wandered over to the sliding glass door that faced the patio.

"I'm luckier than many women, though. If I do decide to sell, at least I have clear title to the house."

"So your only income is what you're making with your teaching?"

Jenna returned to the sofa and tucked her legs under her as she nodded. "It's not that teaching is bad. I honestly enjoy it. It's just that most people don't understand my situation. They get offended when I care about money. I expect East Edge Eddie to charge me more than necessary to repair my car tomorrow, but he still charges me less than the other mechanics in town, Rolf Wyland included. They all assume I'll never know they overcharge, or if I do, I won't care. I have money to burn."

"Sort of like the bad press doctors can get," said Geoff. "People forget that guys like me have just spent ten to twelve years in school and have nothing but debt. Just because they call us 'Doctor,' they think we're rich."

"Have you bought into a partnership with Dr. Rosell?" Jenna asked, glad to change the subject. They had talked enough about her. "You make it sound like you haven't."

Geoff shook his head. "Few men and women today can afford to buy into a practice right out of medical school. Instead, the established physician usually offers you a contract at a salary, usually with an option to buy a partnership after a stated time and upon everyone's approval. I will be Ben Rosell's associate, not his partner. Just paying my malpractice insurance is a great financial burden to me right now."

"Why did you become a doctor?" Jenna asked.

"Probably for the same reason you became a musician. You couldn't do anything else. I have felt for as long as I can remember that God wanted me to be a doctor."

"And you enjoy it?"

Geoff thought carefully. "I don't know if enjoy is the right word. I find it fascinating, challenging, frightening. It stretches me beyond what I would have thought possible. It's given me moments of great joy and great sorrow."

"I wanted to be a concert pianist," Jenna said, "but I'm not quite good enough. It still hurts some days." Jenna blinked in surprise at her words. She'd never even told Tommy that.

"And I want to heal every kid who comes to me," said Geoff. "And I can't. I couldn't even heal my dad." There was pain in his voice, an unexpressed sorrow that Jenna could feel even in the brevity of the words.

"Funny, the chasm between dreams and reality." Jenna's voice was thoughtful. "Learning the difference is maturity, I guess."

"Have you always been such a philosopher?"

"Hardly. But I've learned a lot over the past four to five years. Sometimes I wish I could have done without the pain of the learning, but I know God has taught me things about Himself I'd never have discovered in any other way. And He's given me a group of Christian friends that have supported me when I thought I'd die. And no one has been more special than your sister Janie. She and Arch have been rocks."

Jenna stood up.

"Come on, Geoff. Let's find the kids and take a walk around the reservoir. I don't want to bore you."

Jenna also didn't want to paint herself as a martyr, a poor-little-not-rich girl. Maybe some day when she knew him better, she could tell him more, but not yet. Let him see her whole—or at least not too flawed—before he saw her as fragmented as she had been before time and the Lord had worked their healing.

Suddenly Jenna had a thought. "Do you mind walking where you almost got killed? Will it be too traumatic or something?"

Geoff shook his head. "Don't worry about it. We'll think of it like getting back on a horse after you've been thrown. Besides, what more could possibly happen?"

10

The evening was lovely, soft and warm. Geoff, Jenna and the kids crossed the street in front of the house and began slowly walking along the south shore of the reservoir toward the country club. The tall evergreens towering overhead had been placed there as saplings during the Depression by men working on a WPA project. Now a light breeze soughed through their needles.

On the water floated two pairs of mallards trailing ducklings, a pair of elegant white swans, and, down by the clubhouse, a flock of Canada geese. Overhead swallows darted, and redwinged blackbirds sat lightly on the tall marsh grasses.

Mikey kept himself busy throwing stones into the water, and Libby was his servant, fetching him missiles upon command.

At the small bridge over the feeder creek, near where Geoff had seen the body being dumped, two boys were fishing enthusiastically, if unsuccessfully, ignoring the No Fishing sign to their left. A few other fishermen could be dimly seen on the far wooded banks of the reservoir, their rods flashing in the setting sun. On the golf course some golfers were still chipping and putting, though shortly they were going to need fluorescent balls.

Jenna and Geoff walked slowly. While Jenna looked about her as if she couldn't get enough of the scenery, she was extremely conscious of the man beside her. She felt ridiculous. She also felt somehow reborn, alive in a way she hadn't felt for at least two years.

"So Janie's been a good friend?" Geoff asked, his voice blending softly with the evening's peace.

Jenna smiled at the numerous memories that surfaced.

"When Tommy was first beginning to drink so heavily, I didn't know what to do. I'm from a Christian family where drinking was never considered an option. I had no background in handling problems of such magnitude. I needed someone to talk to. Unfortunately, Mom and Dad live in Montana and here I was in Pennsylvania. We'd only been in this house a few months, and we'd had no opportunity to get to know people. I was trying to hang on alone and getting closer and closer to the edge.

"I went to Calvary Church regularly, but Tommy no longer would go. Because I didn't know how to explain his absence without damaging his reputation, I kept a very low profile.

"One Saturday night, Tommy didn't come home at all. It was the first time. I went to church the next morning not knowing where he was or even if he was all right, imagining all kinds of things. I never heard a word the pastor said because I was too busy praying.

"That afternoon Tommy showed up, and there was the cliched lipstick on his collar.

"I went to church that evening because I had to get out

of the house. I put Mikey and Libby in the nursery and walked down the hall to the sanctuary. Suddenly the man in front of me stopped, turned abruptly and slammed right into me. The only reason I didn't fall over was because he pushed me shoulder first into a door jamb.

"Normally, I would have laughed off a collision like that. That evening I burst into tears.

"The man was Arch, and he stared at me open-mouthed, appalled at what he thought he'd done. Janie was with him. She just put her arm around me, pushed me into an empty room beside us, and held me while I sobbed and sobbed."

Jenna giggled. "I can still see Arch's horrified face. Poor man. When they found out I lived down the hill from them, they made me their project. Janie would stop in to visit. They had Mikey and me and, later, Libby for meals. Archie came down a couple of times when Tommy got abusive. Janie took me to the women's Bible study and the women's fellowship meetings. She introduced me as her neighbor Jenna, not as Tommy Mathisson's wife. And she listened and loved and counseled."

Jenna could feel Geoff's eyes on her.

"Are you the friend that kept Zach and Tim and Patsy when our father died last year?" he asked. "I remember Janie saying a friend took care of the kids and made it possible for her and Arch to spend so much time with Dad near the end."

Jenna nodded. "It was a hard time for Janie."

"For all of us," said Geoff. "Mom died when I was in college, but it was quickly, in an accident. Watching Dad die was agonizing. Here I was, a doctor, and I could do nothing."

They walked in silence for awhile, reached the clubhouse, turned, and began walking back toward Jenna's.

"You know," said Jenna, "when I think of Tommy and his rebellion and his death, I think of the consequences of his actions, not just for him, but for the three of us. It's made me so aware that you can't act in a vacuum.

"When your dad died, he didn't willfully choose that course. Death is a part of life. It hurts. It changes our lives in ways we couldn't even imagine. But Tommy's death—"

When Jenna fell silent, Geoff spoke. "It's the knowledge that his actions were willfully wrong, and the hurt was avoidable that's hard to deal with?"

Jenna felt grateful that he understood. "When you showed up last night and scared me to death, I got mad at Tommy because he had left me to be alone in a situation like that. I thought I had grown beyond that feeling, but every so often it leaps out and smacks me. I have to be careful I don't get angry at him all over again."

"I think many widows and widowers get mad at their spouses for dying on them," said Geoff. "The pain, the unknown, the inconvenience, all cause anger. But when the death could have been avoided, the anger must be greater."

"Probably," said Jenna. "And while it might be natural to feel that anger, it's wrong to hang on to it. It's unhealthy. It's ungodly. And it's a constant struggle. I think I'm doing well, and then something happens to kindle it again."

"Like having strange men pass out on your back porch."

"Well, at least that hasn't been all bad. He turned out to know about jumper cables."

Geoff chuckled, then turned as Mikey shouted.

"Hey, Mom, look what I found!"

The kids had wandered back to the bridge over the feeder creek. A pile of stones had been stockpiled on the bridge to toss into the water for one great frenzy of splashing. As they had scurried between the water and the bridge, sliding down the bank on their seats, crawling up on their hands and knees, pockets loaded with stones, they had gotten muddier and mussier and happier.

"Look what I've found," Mikey yelled again from under the bridge.

"Geoff!" Jenna's heart beat erratically as terrible visions leaped to her mind. "He couldn't have found another . . . ?"

"Of course not," Geoff answered firmly, but he ran to Mikey just as quickly as Jenna.

"Look!" shouted Mikey.

He was standing just under the bridge, pointing at his feet. Beside him Libby was jumping up and down with excitement.

"It's a treasure," yelled Mikey. At his feet was a dirty, old shoe box.

"A treasure!" echoed Libby.

Jenna and Geoff looked at each other with relief. This "treasure" looked perfectly acceptable.

Mikey said, "It was under that bunch of rocks." He pointed to a small mound of stones. "Libby and me were collecting them and we found this box buried there against the side of the bridge. It's a buried treasure! A real buried treasure!"

"Did my nephew Zach ever show you the treasure he found in the reservoir?" Geoff asked Mikey as he picked up the box.

"This is better than Zach's," said Mikey. "It's heavier."

As the kids reached for the box, Geoff lifted it into the air.

"Listen, guys," he said to their upturned faces. "I expect us to find jewelry that's been stolen or something like that. Do you know what that means? That means we can't keep it."

"But I found it!" protested Mikey.

"What if someone took your bike and someone else found it? Wouldn't you want them to give it back to you?"

Mikey nodded resignedly. "Yes."

"Okay?" asked Geoff.

"Okay. I have to give it back." Suddenly his face brightened. "But maybe they'll give me a reward!"

"Greedy wretch," said Jenna as Geoff lowered the box and the kids pulled it open.

"Plastic bags," said Mikey disgustedly, pawing hurriedly through the box. "Plastic bags and plastic bags and *more* plastic bags." He made a little pile.

Geoff opened one of the small, silver colored envelopes. He looked startled.

"What is it?" asked Jenna.

"Run home and call the police, Jenna. It's a cache of drugs."

11

Jenna, Mikey, and Libby stood off to the side and watched the activity. Police milled about, Paul Janczyn in charge. Patrolman Monihan looked over and waved a friendly hand, much to the evident displeasure of the lieutenant. He scowled, apparently at such a show of comraderie toward people who were creating more work for him than they ought.

"Come here, son," the lieutenant called to Mikey. His voice was easy, not showing the testiness evident when he talked with the adults.

Mikey walked to the policeman, and Jenna went with him.

"Show me where you found the box and how, Mikey," the lieutenant said. "And I'm very interested in anything you have to tell me."

With great dignity and care, Mikey described his and Libby's rock gathering and the resultant discovery of the shoe box.

"Was it buried in a hole?" asked Lt. Janczyn.

Mikey shook his head. "No. It was just sort of leaning

against the bridge with a bunch of rocks piled over it and weeds around it."

"Was the bottom wet at all?"

Mikey shook his head. "It was back from the edge of the stream and it was resting on a couple of rocks to keep its bottom dry. I bet if it was there during a big rainstorm, it would get wet. The creek would rise and the stuff would get ruined."

"Did anyone ever suggest to you that you might find a treasure buried under the bridge?"

Mikey looked at the lieutenant in surprise. "Of course not."

"Thank you, son. You and your mom can go while I talk with Dr. McGregor." The lieutenant stuck out his hand and Mikey shook it with great aplomb.

"Let's go watch from the bridge," suggested Jenna. "We can see what's going on without being in the way."

They clambered up the bank and leaned over the rail. Mikey stood beside Jenna, his chest threatening to split his T-shirt so puffed was it with pride.

"You did a fine job, Mikey," Jenna said. "You answered all the lieutenant's questions very well. I was proud of you."

"I told them everything I could think of," Mikey said.

Libby looked at her big brother with awe. All her life she had assumed that Mikey knew everything, a supposition he had done nothing to counter. Now with the imprimatur of the police upon him, Mikey was truly infallible. Jenna imagined that Libby saw a halo shining over Mikey's all too human brow.

"What are they going to do with the stuff?" Libby asked,

utterly confident Mikey knew.

"Take it to the police station," he answered. "It's evidence."

She nodded, obviously not sure what "evidence" was, but awed by Mikey's tone of authority. "But how did the drugs get there, Mikey?"

Mikey shrugged. "Some bad guys, Lib. Maybe the same guys who chased Dr. McGregor last night."

Libby's eyes grew round. "Will they chase us now?"

"Nah," said Mikey assuredly. "The police already have the stuff, so we're safe."

So much for worrying that he might be scared by all that was happening.

Suddenly Jenna knew the three of them were not alone on the bridge. She smelled a fourth.

She spun around and looked into the grizzled and unnervingly close face of Charlie Wino. The man had on the same clothes he'd worn that afternoon—was it only that afternoon?—when she'd seen him at The Lighthouse. What she hadn't appreciated then because of distance between them and the strong aroma of pine disinfectant was the ripe odor Charlie exuded.

Instinctively, Jenna felt threatened by the man. It might have been the way he stood, leaning forward, invading her air space, or the way he scowled, or his slovenly manner of dress. Whichever, Jenna backed up a step and looked over the bridge to remind herself that Geoff, Lt. Janczyn, and Patrolman Monihan were only a shout away.

Mikey, however, wasn't the least bit put off by the man.

"Hey, Charlie Wino, guess what? We found some drugs!"

The man scowled at Mikey. "What did you call me?"

Jenna longed to grab the boy and push him behind her where Libby was hiding. But Mikey had thought about the man so often and been so fascinated by him that he assumed he and the man shared a friendship.

"Charlie Wino," repeated Mikey. "That's your name."

Charlie Wino stared at the boy for a moment, then began to laugh, a deep wheezing noise that gurgled up from his stomach. In that instant he looked less frightening, almost approachable. But only for that instant. Then he scratched his belly and belched, looked Jenna in the eye and grinned insolently.

She saw he delighted in offending, and she tried to look neutral. She must have succeeded because he turned back to Mikey.

"So you found drugs, did you?"

"Under the bridge buried in some stones," said Mikey in excitement.

"Was there a lot?" asked Charlie.

Mikey nodded. "Lots and lots of little silver bags."

"Did you count how many?"

"Lots."

"Did you ever see anyone fooling around under the bridge before?"

"Oh, sure, lots of times," said Mikey.

That alert, intelligent look that Charlie tried to hide flashed through his eyes. "Who?"

"Me and Timmy and Zach. And Georgie who lives over there." He pointed to a house down the road past his own. "And some big guys from East Edge come out here to fish a lot."

With relief Jenna saw Geoff climbing up the bank. Charlie also saw him and scowled.

Abruptly he leaned close to Jenna. She tried to pull back but the railing of the bridge held her. She felt the heat of his unwashed body, the menace of his harsh voice.

"A piece of advice, lady. Stay out of things that don't concern you! And keep your kids out!"

With that he turned and shambled away, throwing a sour glance at the police who were preparing to leave.

Jenna shivered.

"Bye, Charlie Wino," yelled Mikey, waving madly.

Charlie did not acknowledge the boy.

"Where are his bags, Mom?" asked Mikey as he watched his friend disappear. "He always carries his bags with his stuff in them. He doesn't have them tonight."

As Lt. Janczyn and Geoff approached, Jenna wondered about Charlie's empty hands. Had they planned to collect a treasure after dark? Certainly someone had planned to come for the drugs. Was it Charlie? Had he been one of the men Geoff had interrupted last night?

But if he were the man Geoff had seen in the porch light at Tidbit's house, wouldn't he have recognized Charlie? He was certainly distinctive enough. But the loss of blood, shock and exhaustion had taken their toll. It was possible he couldn't remember even someone as unique as Charlie.

Or maybe Charlie was the man who stayed behind, the one who finished disposing of the body. Had he also hidden the drugs? If so, would he hold it against Mikey that the boy had found them? She had read that drug dealers weren't particularly stable. In fact, they were very violent.

And violent men try to kill people by any means available, even white cars.

She shivered.

But why hide the drugs in the first place? There must be tremendous street value in the contents of those silver plastic pouches. It was hard to believe that anyone would let that treasure out of their hands, especially clever Charlie.

Of course, the men with the body hadn't known who Geoff was last night. He could have been the vanguard of a team of police or Drug Enforcement Agency men. Or of a rival gang which might well be more dangerous than any number of law enforcement personnel. Or he could have been one of Bobby Coe's friends come to even the score. Or maybe they thought their identities were known, and it was imperative that the drugs not be found on them or in their car.

For whatever reason, temporarily ridding themselves of the drugs must have seemed absolutely pressing, absolutely necessary. They must have tried to hide them where no one would find them and planned to come get them tonight or as soon as the area was quiet again.

Of course, they couldn't have anticipated that a kid collecting stones would wander along.

Jenna realized she was assuming that the drugs and the body and the white car were connected somehow. Certainly there weren't two or three sets of criminals, were there? One for the body and one for the drugs and one for the white car?

Libby had remained behind Jenna's legs, arms wrapped tightly around her right knee, peering around her right leg. Mikey leaned against her left side.

Lt. Janczyn looked at the cozy family picture and ran his hand through his curly hair in exasperation.

"Just when I started to believe Dr. McGregor was only a

doctor who likes to jog dangerously late and you're only a lady who doesn't like the clutter of bodies on her patio, you both show up again. And again. And together every time. Why?"

Jenna stared at him a moment, trying to think of an answer. None came.

"I thought you told me you didn't know each other," the lieutenant said, sounding for all the world like he'd caught them in a major lie.

"We didn't before last night," Jenna said.

Lt. Janczyn nodded skeptically, and Jenna felt anger stir. She wasn't used to being doubted.

"You knew those drugs were there, didn't you, Mrs. Mathisson?" he barked suddenly, pointing to the bridge. "For some reason you wanted them found."

"I beg your pardon." Jenna hoped she sounded as offended as she felt.

"You decided to let the boy find them and therefore appear innocent."

"Are you serious, Lieutenant?" Jenna was indignant. "If what you say were somehow true, that I did know about the drugs, do you think I'd let my child become part of a criminal matter? What kind of a mother do you think I am?"

Lt. Janczyn sighed. "Relax, Mrs. Mathisson. I have no reason to suspect you're anything more than an innocent bystander who somehow got wrapped up in a situation beyond your ken. Same with the doctor. But I've got to ask questions and make certain. That's my job. I'll take that list you made for me of everyone you saw this afternoon."

He pocketed the paper without looking at it, nodded farewell, and walked slowly to his car and the waiting

Patrolman Monihan. On the way he popped a handful of Tums. Jenna wondered if they were necessitated by Geoff and her or by Eager Beaver Monihan.

She looked down the length of the reservoir, gleaming silver in the lowering darkness. It was achingly beautiful. Overhead, bats flew erratic patterns above the water and across the stillness a screech owl sounded. A bullfrog croaked his bassy ribbit at her feet and cricket sounds filled the air.

And somehow, someplace in this peaceful, beautiful setting, Jenna knew that there was evil—and that it was slowly wrapping its vicious arms around her and her children.

12

At home again, Jenna finally got the kids quieted down and to bed, though it took some time to subdue Mikey's enthusiasm for crime solving. He was ready to enlist under Lt. Janczyn tomorrow.

"All I ask is that you graduate from high school first," said Jenna as she tucked the lightweight blanket under his chin.

"What's high school?" asked Mikey.

"Where the big kids go."

He thought about it for a moment, then shrugged. "If you think I ought to."

When she returned to the living room, she found Geoff reading the Philadelphia *Inquirer*. The sight of him looking so comfortable and so right in the sole chair with Lump and Midget sleeping at his feet made her catch her breath.

He put the paper aside and turned his attention to her. He was here because she had asked him to stay. It had seemed so important to tell him about Charlie Wino's threat.

In her confusion over her strong emotional response to this man she scarcely knew, Jenna turned to the one place she always felt at home. She ran off some chords to loosen her fingers, then moved into Beethoven's *Pathetique Sonata*. Tension and uncertainty washed away like a sand castle before the flowing tide as she lost herself in the somber music.

Then she moved into the fast and flashy *Prelude and Fugue in B Flat Major* by Bach. Not only were there serious things in her life like unpaid bills and bodies that went with the Beethoven; there were hopeful things like Geoff and her kids that went with the Bach piece.

When she finished, Geoff spoke.

"I thought you said you weren't good enough to be a concert pianist."

She smiled. He certainly could say the nicest things. "I'm not. I'm just good enough to impress people—which does have its advantages."

"I've got to tell you that I've been suitably impressed, and by more than just your piano playing."

Jenna was afraid the corners of her mouth were in her ears, her smile was so broad. She began to hope Geoff liked transparent women. "Let's sit in the den. There are enough seats for both of us in there."

Relaxing on the sofa with iced tea and some pretzels, Jenna related her experience with Charlie Wino.

"There's just something about him that doesn't ring true," she said. "I don't know what it is, but he's not what he appears."

"I think you should tell Janczyn both what he said and what you think," said Geoff.

"Really? Do you honestly think Janczyn cares about

what Charlie said, let alone what I think?"

"If he's a good cop he does. And even though he's not about to win any personality awards, there's no reason to doubt his ability at his work."

"But he gave you such a hard time."

"As well he should have," said Geoff. "You must admit, my story is unique."

Jenna smiled. "That's a polite word for it."

"Janczyn needs your information, Jenna, because he can't risk that that crazy derelict is more than he appears. He's got to find out whether the murderers are connected with the drug cache. And he's got to ascertain whether Charlie is connected with either or both. I definitely think you should talk to Janczyn."

The concern in his eyes comforted Jenna. "If you think I should."

"I do."

Jenna nodded and reached for the phone. It wasn't that she couldn't make up her mind to call Janczyn herself. She'd been making up her mind all by herself about far more important things for the past few years. She was just enjoying the great luxury of bouncing an idea off an interested person who was as involved in the situation as she, relishing the privilege of getting the opinion of someone over six years of age.

Not for the first time she pondered the changes in herself since Tommy's death. Actually his absences and financial irresponsibility had forced her to stretch painfully even before he accidentally killed himself. Since then she had become even more independent and capable. Tommy wouldn't even recognize her. Gone was the quiet, whatever-you-want-dear woman he had married. In her place had developed an opinionated, strong woman forged in the traumatic fires of widowhood and fiscal stress.

She glanced at Geoff from under her lashes. Would he prove to be more than a match for her newfound strength? It would be interesting to see.

"Why have you never married?" she asked suddenly, Lt. Janczyn forgotten.

He looked at her searchingly, as if trying to discern why she asked.

"I almost married once, about my second year in medical school. She was a nice girl, a fine Christian. Amy. We went to college together. But we both realized it wouldn't have worked."

He shook his head. "That's not quite what I mean. It would have worked in that we would have remained married all our lives. We both believed in that commitment. And we wouldn't have been miserable. Like I said, she was very nice, a considerate, caring woman. But there would have been no intimacy beyond physical. We realized that we would have been just two people living in the same house, not 'as one'."

Jenna nodded. She often found herself wondering, in retrospect, at what appeared to be the shallowness of her marriage even before Tommy hurt his knee. They had been merely two people in one house, one who called all the shots and one who did everything she was told. If Tommy hadn't changed so dramatically, would she have remained so pliable and willing to be manipulated all her life? Jenna shook her head at the unanswerable question.

Jenna knew that if she married again, she would need a

man strong enough to give her more fully developed personality room to continue flowering, a man who wasn't threatened by her desire to remain a person in her own right. She cherished the thought of working through the biblical principles of a husband's headship and a wife's submission with such a man.

"I'm just waiting for the right woman," said Geoff. "And I admit I'm being fussy." He smiled right into her eyes. "But I have great hopes. Now you'd better call Lt. Janczyn."

She dialed with a shaking finger.

"I'd like to speak with Lt. Janczyn, please," she told the man at the other end of the wire in a breathless voice. She swallowed and cleared her throat.

In no time she had repeated her conversation with Charlie to Lt. Janczyn who noted the information with his usual grace.

"You should have told me right away, Mrs. Mathisson," he complained.

"You're welcome, Lieutenant. Calling you specially was no trouble."

"Yeah," he said. "Thanks." And he hung up.

"So much for the lieutenant thinking much of my thoughts," she said.

"Well, Charlie's my main suspect," said Geoff, standing up to leave.

"Charlie's our only suspect," pointed out Jenna. "We don't know anyone else who by the remotest stretch of imagination might be involved."

"I wish I could remember what the man I saw looked like. It's so frustrating!" He ran his fingers through his thick, dark hair. "I keep trying, but nothing comes to mind. In fact, the harder I try, the blanker my mind seems. I want to be able to look at police mug shots or talk with a police artist or something. I feel so useless right now."

"Don't struggle with it. Just let the memory perk to the surface in its own good time."

Jenna walked Geoff to the door.

"I'll stop for you tomorrow at noon to take your car to Eddie's."

"I'll be ready. I hope you beat Rolf at golf."

Geoff just laughed as he waved good-bye.

Jenna wandered slowly through the house making all the little nightly checks of the doors and windows and lights and electrical appliances. Her last checks were the kids' rooms. As was her nightly habit, she stood over each child and prayed for God's keeping and protection.

She climbed into her bed, a Dick Franklin mystery in her hand. She definitely needed something to turn off her mind, and the snappy action of her favorite author ought to do the trick.

Half an hour later, the shrill and unexpected bleat of the phone shattered the stillness. She jumped and reluctantly put Mr. Francis aside. As she stared at the instrument on the table beside the bed, it bleated at her again. She hated late night calls. She always feared it would be her mother saying her father had had a heart attack or her father saying her mother had had an accident.

Willing her heart to quiet down, she lifted the receiver and said, "Hello?"

Silence answered her.

"Hello?" she said again.

"We're going to get you, you know."

The whispered statement slithered out of the phone into Jenna's ear. She blanched and her heart began to pound again.

"We're going to get both of you."

There was a click and the line went dead, but Jenna continued to hold the receiver. She felt paralyzed and very, very vulnerable.

How does he know who I am? How does he know my number? Dear Father, what should I do? Help me!

Her mind slowly began to function again. "Both of you" the voice had said. She and Geoff.

Her breath caught in her throat. Not the kids. Surely he didn't mean any threat to the kids. He'd have said "all of you" if he meant that, wouldn't he?

Dear Father, not the kids!

Jenna threw back the covers and ran to the children's rooms. She began to breathe again when she satisfied herself that they were sleeping peacefully and naturally.

Not the kids.

Slowly and carefully, tiptoeing even though there was no one to hear her, Jenna went from window to window, room to room, looking outside, checking locks, repeatedly telling herself she was safe. No one could harm her here in her own home.

"We're going to get you."

She shivered violently and wished she had the nerve, and the right, to call Geoff. Maybe he had gotten a phone call too.

She shook her head. He hadn't gotten one. Nobody knew how to reach him except her and Lt. Janczyn. Jenna Mathisson was easy to look up in the phone book, but there was no Geoffrey McGregor listed.

The phone suddenly rang again. Jenna stared at it, mesmerized by waves of danger she imagined flowing from it.

Don't answer! she told herself.

You've got to! she argued. *What if it's a legitimate, middle-of-the-night emergency?*

"Hello?" She hated the tremor in her voice while at the same time she was proud that she could speak at all.

"Hello, Harriet, can I speak to Dolly?"

"I beg your pardon?"

"Isn't this Harriet? Isn't Dolly there?"

"Sorry," said Jenna as relief flooded her. "No Harriets here. No Dollys either."

Jenna had barely removed her hand from the phone when it rang again. She grabbed it.

"Hello. There's no Harriet or Dolly here."

"Of course not," breathed a malicious voice. "Just you. And we'll get you. Both of you."

Jenna left the receiver lying on the floor where she dropped it and ran for her bedroom. She sat huddled against the headboard, staring vacantly at the Dick Franklin novel by her side. His heroines probably wouldn't cower like her, but then they weren't real people either.

When dawn began lightening the sky, Jenna finally fell asleep.

13

Jenna was outside playing catch with the kids when Geoff arrived. She looked at him with dark, haunted eyes.

"You look like you had a bad night," he said as he climbed out of his car and pushed Abraham, the Steagers' huge Newfoundland, back in. Abraham responded by hanging out the driver's window and drooling down the side of the car.

Lump and Midget sat on a windowsill in the safety of the house, hissing and howling at Abraham who ignored them. In fact, Jenna doubted he could even hear the cats over the noise of his panting.

As Geoff handed her the clothes he had borrowed, he cupped her chin in his hand and turned her face to the sun. He ran a finger over the circles that stained the flesh beneath her eyes.

Her control almost shattered by his caring touch, she said simply, "Threatening phone calls," and explained her late night vigil to the startled man.

"It's my fault," Geoff said as she finished. "Because they

don't know how to get hold of me, they're harassing you. Have you told the police?"

Jenna nodded. "Early this morning. Not that they can do anything."

Obviously distressed, Geoff began working on Jenna's car, connecting the jumper cables to the terminals of his and Jenna's batteries. On the second try her engine turned over. After he collected the cables and stowed them in his trunk, he turned to Jenna.

"Maybe this will cheer you up. Rolf has invited us to be his guests for dinner tonight at the country club. I told him you were already committed to the Narduccis, and he said to bring them along too, all of us as his guests. He even offered Valerie as babysitter."

An evening out with friends! It sounded wonderful and Jenna was more than glad to say yes, more than glad to tuck all the strange and frightening happenings of the past two days out of mind.

"Just remember, you're with me and we're with Rolf," said Geoff. "Everything will be fine."

All the way to Tolys to drop off the kids, Jenna smiled. All the way into East Edge, under the Route 30 bypass, past Rolf's gas station where she beeped at Harley who was pumping gas, past Calvary Church, all the way to East Edge Eddie's, Jenna smiled. Even when Eddie told her he couldn't get her car finished before three o'clock, she smiled.

A date. For goodness sakes, she had a date. Wouldn't her mother laugh if she knew? Wouldn't Janie love it if she knew?

"Eddie, not until three o'clock?"

"I hope."

"Eddie, you're driving me crazy. I need my car!"

"I won't go home today until it's done, I promise, Mrs. Mathisson."

"Now, I'm trusting you, Eddie."

But a little question kept popping up at the back of her mind. When she got her car back, would she lose contact with Geoff? Maybe he was only being polite, chauffeuring her around. After all, she had experienced some pretty frightening things because of him. He might just feel obligated.

But he hadn't sounded obligated last night or even a few minutes ago. Had he?

She walked over to Geoff's car, thankful he and Abraham had followed her into town.

"Not until 3:00," she said.

"You don't want to wait, do you?" he asked.

She shook her head. "I need to go to the church and make certain everything's ready for tonight."

"I'll take you."

He helped her transfer the programs and other supplies from her car to his and from the car to the church while Abraham barked his encouragement. Geoff tied him to a tree in the church yard with a rope he found in the trunk.

"If the dog ever decides to protest being tied and gives even a slight tug, he's free."

Abraham chose not to protest but rather to lie in the shade and grab a nap. This two weeks that the Steager kids were at the shore were his vacation, too.

Calvary Church was a perfect size for the recital. It seated about 200 and Jenna expected 100-125, enough people not to look lost in the auditorium yet scattered enough to be comfortable on a hot night.

"Do you need an usher to hand out programs?" Geoff asked as he placed them neatly on a counter in the vestibule.

"Mikey considers that his job and Libby insists on helping, but I'd love an overseer."

"You've got one."

By 1:30 all the preparations for the recital and reception were completed. The pink, lavender, and white flowers sat on the piano. The punch was stored in the refrigerator downstairs. Jenna's pink linen tablecloth covered the serving table, and on it was a second, smaller floral arrangement of pink, lavender, and white bracketed by silver candlesticks and pink candles. Lavender paper plates and napkins sat in neat stacks next to the spot reserved for the cake, and plastic cups waited next to an empty punch bowl.

"I've got to remember matches," Jenna muttered, writing herself a note. "And more ice."

"Where can we go for a ride?" Geoff asked as he untied Abraham. "It seems like a waste of a lovely afternoon to just go home. I'll be a tourist and you can take me sight-seeing."

"How about south along Route 82?" Jenna suggested, surprisingly happy that he wanted to spend more time with her.

They drove slowly among the low, rolling hills of southern Chester County. They passed fields where great flocks of Canada geese wandered, tearing up the sod. Scores of awkward goslings trailed behind their parents as they foraged. Occasional horses could be seen wandering slowly over enclosed meadows. Herds of cattle also appeared, cattle egrets standing on their backs or stalking beside them.

Abraham, leaning out the open rear window, ears flapping in the breeze, greeted them all joyfully.

"Much of this land used to be part of the King Ranch," Jenna said. "There were great herds of cattle flown in from Texas each spring to fatten on the rich pasture. Every fall there was a round-up with cowboys, just like out West. But the ranch is gone, and the area's protected from development under the Brandywine Conservency."

Horse farms, crisp and clean, spread out around them as they neared Unionville. They drove under a canopy of mighty trees that stretched in an arch of green over their heads.

"This is my favorite part of the road," said Jenna as they drove through the emerald tunnel.

Geoff turned off onto a side road and for some time they drove without any destination, enjoying the silence. They stopped the car to watch a horse being schooled in jumps, but it was obvious that Abraham was a major distraction to both horse and rider.

"Things are so peaceful here that it's hard to remember the chaos of the last couple of days," said Geoff as they drove on. "This is much more to my liking."

When they approached a covered bridge, Geoff pulled off the road. The brilliant summer sun bathed everything in a warm golden glow.

"Look at that, will you? An honest to goodness covered bridge!"

"There are still a few of them on these back roads," said Jenna.

The old wooden bridge spanned a broad creek. It

resembled a long, narrow house with a very broad doorway and was just wide enough for one car to pass through at a time.

"These old bridges came in handy in the days of horse travel," Jenna commented. "If a rider got caught in a storm, he could wait it out in the shelter of a covered bridge."

They got out and exclaimed over the date of 1859 inscribed on the bridge's lintel. They walked into the structure. Standing in the center, Geoff looked up. The roof had a few holes in it, but it could obviously still offer protection to anyone caught in the rain. The sides were also largely intact, though here and there a slat was missing.

They exited on the far side.

"Come on," Geoff said. "Let's walk along the stream."

They wandered slowly beside the water while Abraham, smiling broadly, ran on ahead. Jenna watched the creek jump over some rocks, then deepen to flow silently between its banks. Rocks of all sizes lay beside the stream, some large enough to sit on, others just right for throwing. Jenna picked up a small stone and tossed it into the water. It splashed beautifully.

"Now I know where your kids get their passion for rock throwing," Geoff said.

"Rocks and water go together," she said and laughed as he tossed a couple of his own.

"I've been thinking about our conversation on consequences," Geoff said as they walked on downstream. "Pehaps one of the most difficult things about living with them is that they are constant reminders of things we'd like to forget."

Jenna tried unsuccessfully to skip a rock across the creek. She nodded.

"Every time I try to balance my checkbook and come out in the red, I have to fight getting mad at Tommy all over again. Or when I look at you and see that wound, I get angry at the man who caused it." She reached out to touch the still-angry weal on the side of his head, then quickly stuck her hand in her jeans pocket, shocked at herself for being so familiar. Geoff didn't seem to mind at all.

"It's important to remember, though," he added, "that consequences result from good as well as wrong actions. How about Tommy's knee? It was just an accident that it was so badly damaged. Accidents happen every day.

"Or take the kids I see, especially at Children's Hospital. Many are quite ill, some will even die. Usually no one did anything to cause that illness. It just happened as part of living. But because there are such dramatic consequences, there is also the opportunity to become and remain angry or bitter."

"Or guilty," said Jenna. "Sal Narducci was telling me about his brother Nick. He OD'ed, but it was Sal who introduced him to drugs."

Geoff whistled between his teeth. "That's a rough memory to deal with. There's got to be a special pain when you know it was your actions, inadvertent or not, that created such serious consequences for another. Lots of Christians don't do very well with guilt. I've always wondered how I'd handle it if I ever hit a kid with my car."

"And there are always the memories, the regrets," said Jenna, "for those who cause them and those who receive them."

119

Geoff picked up a stone and skipped it four times.

"How did you do that?" Jenna demanded. She grabbed a rock and tried to skip it. It sank immediately.

"It's all in the flick of the wrist." Geoff demonstrated with another four-skipper. He reached for a third flat rock at the water's edge and lost his footing on the slick mud. He gave a mighty whoop and ended up with one leg in the water to his thigh and the other on the bank.

He looked through the water at his once-white tennis shoe as his foot disappeared beneath the silt settling over it.

"The consequences of stepping in the water are wet feet and very dirty sneakers," he said pontifically. "My choice of reactions is anger or laughter."

"Or taking your shoes off and dangling your feet," said Jenna with a laugh. She climbed onto a large nearby rock and followed her own advice. "Wow, this is chilly! The sun fools you. You forget it's still early in the season. And if you fall in here," she swept her arm in a large semi-circle, indicating the area in front of her rock, "you'll go in to your waist!"

Geoff pulled himself out of the creek and joined her, placing his wet sock and shoe in the sun to dry.

"You know another thing about consequences?" asked Jenna, returning to their serious conversation. "They aren't fair. What did Tommy do to deserve a bad knee? What have the little kids you see ever done to deserve all that pain? If fair—from our perspective—were the way things worked, Tommy's knee would have lasted forever or only really bad kids would get sick. But God's idea of what's best for us and our idea of what's fair are sometimes very different. Tommy never understood that."

Geoff lifted his face to the sun. "Anger, bitterness, guilt—or acceptance, forgiveness, godliness. It's our choice."

"And it's a choice Tommy couldn't see. He dwelt on all the negatives."

"And you didn't," said Geoff. "You came through a terrible circumstance lovelier than ever."

Jenna flushed with pleasure. "How do you know? You never knew me then."

Geoff just smiled.

Abraham came running toward them, tongue flapping in the breeze, feathers wet from the creek. He obviously planned to join them on their rock. He just as obviously wouldn't fit.

Jenna reached to stop him at the same time a loud crack rent the air and a small geyser of water shot upward in front of them.

For a frozen moment Jenna couldn't move even though her stunned mind recognized the noise for what it was—a gunshot.

14

"Down, Jenna!" yelled Geoff.

Not needing to be told, Jenna threw herself facedown beside him on their rock.

"Hey, Whoever-you-are!" yelled Geoff to the sky. "There are people here! And this most certainly isn't hunting season!"

Jenna lifted her head and looked cautiously around. The stream continued to bubble benignly by; the field was quiet and empty, and the covered bridge, washed in sunlight and distance, looked like a watercolor painting. Their car and another were parked beside the bridge.

"Geoff, there's a white car behind ours by the bridge, and its trunk is up."

Geoff rolled over and looked where she indicated.

"He must know there are people here," Geoff said in disgust. "Unless . . . ."

"Unless he's shooting at us on purpose," Jenna finished fearfully.

As if to affirm her conclusion, another shot rang out. A rock scarcely a foot from Jenna's head shattered, sending a fragment slicing across the back of her knuckles.

Geoff grabbed her by the waist and pulled her after him into the water. A third shot struck the top of the rock where they had been.

"Crouch down behind the rock," he told her. "The shots are coming from the covered bridge. If we can stay low enough, the rock will hide us. I think."

Jenna shivered violently as the cold water closed over her shoulders. The water was too deep for her to kneel, too shallow for her to stand. She crouched, hugging the base of the rock and praying that her head didn't show over the top of it.

She pulled her injured hand out of the water and looked at the cut inflicted by the ricocheting fragment. Blood crept along the line of the cut, but it was obvious that the wound wasn't deep. She felt a surge of relief. Because she was a pianist, healthy hands were of paramount importance.

Geoff crouched beside her, arm still about her waist, back pressed against the stream bank.

Abraham barked wildly and ran back and forth along the bank. Something was wrong. He didn't know what it was, but he certainly didn't like it. He walked into the water to his elbows and backed out. He climbed onto the rock they were hiding behind and lay down, his head hanging over until he was eyeball to eyeball with Jenna.

"Are you all right, Jenna?" Geoff asked.

"Scared to death, but fine," she said. "What's going on?"

"I don't know," Geoff said. "But somehow this has to be connected to Thursday night and last night."

"A consequence, huh?"

Geoff gave a short bark of laughter and wrapped his arm more tightly about her waist.

A fourth shot rang out and Abraham took a flying leap into the water. Jenna and Geoff tried not to choke as the wash from the dog's landing splashed over them. Jenna sputtered as she swallowed some of the muddy water and had a coughing attack. Geoff cupped her chin in his hand to keep it above the water until she recovered.

He then turned to look cautiously toward the bridge. "We've got to figure out how to get out of here soon or hyperthermia will get us if Abraham doesn't drown us first."

The huge beast swam to Jenna and tried to climb in her lap. She felt her balance slipping, and but for Geoff's arm, would have fallen.

"No, Abraham, no!" She pushed the great beast away and he moved to Geoff who, able to kneel, had no lap for the dog to climb on.

"Stand up, you big oaf," Geoff instructed as he pushed Abraham away. "You can probably touch the bottom with no trouble."

Instead, Abraham swam away from them and began paddling with the current toward the bridge.

"Geoff, he'll get hurt!" Jenna screamed. "He'll get shot!"

She made a move to go after him, but Geoff tightened his hold on her waist and held her behind the rock.

"Stay here," he told her.

She watched the big, black dog fearfully, shivering as much in apprehension as cold.

"Look!" Geoff exclaimed suddenly. "It'll be all right! Here comes a car!"

Jenna looked out from behind the rock to see a blue station wagon approaching from the south. "And there goes our man!"

They stood to watch a slim figure silhouetted against the brilliant afternoon sun run to the white car behind theirs, throw something long and slender in the trunk and drive quickly away. Almost immediately the station wagon drove across the bridge, followed by a large, multi-windowed RV.

Someone in the RV caught sight of Jenna and Geoff standing in the water and pointed. The vehicle swerved onto the shoulder of the road and six elderly people spilled out. Gesturing excitedly as they walked, they made for the stream. Once there, they took their shoes and socks off and began cautiously wading.

"Little do they know that they saved our lives," said Geoff. "And they'll also prevent whoever it was from returning."

Jenna reached for her shoes, still baking in the sun.

"We'd still better go while we can."

Geoff grabbed his shoes, too, and since they were both already wet, they began wading toward the bridge. Mid-stream, though, Jenna stepped in a hole, lost her balance and fell, completely submerging. She rose, spluttering, and Geoff grabbed her elbow to steady her.

"I love coordinated, graceful women," he said.

She ran her hands through her now frizzy curls and laughed. At least there would never be any need for vanity around Geoff. He'd already seen her looking her worst.

When they waded into the shallower water near the bridge, Abraham waited for them, barking his welcome. The people from the RV waved happily. They were boon companions all, sharing a romp in the creek.

As Jenna, Geoff, and Abraham climbed the bank by the bridge, the campers in the water began discreetly kicking water at each other, then throwing handfuls. They laughed delightedly, caught up in their gentle frolic.

The sunlight refracted through the drops flying in the air, making tiny rainbows. The joy and normalcy of the scene made the short, terror-filled moments of the attack all the more bizarre. Jenna stared at the cut on the back of her hand to remind herself it had really happened.

They looked carefully up and down the road before they went to their car, but no one was to be seen.

"Someone must have followed us from town," Jenna said.

"I guess so," agreed Geoff. "I wasn't expecting to be followed, so I never looked. But it's definitely time to visit Lt. Janczyn."

Abraham, having shaken water all over Jenna, Geoff and the car, climbed into the back seat, panting happily. He had had a fine time.

Absorbed in the impact of a world suddenly filled with danger, Geoff and Jenna rode quietly into town.

15

They drove directly to the police station and were buzzed through a locked door to meet a police sergeant in a shaggy common room. He graciously offered them chairs with the stuffings coming out, as he sat on the edge of a desk. "Lt. Janczyn's in a highly important meeting right now and I can't reach him."

"Look," demanded Geoff, "we were just shot at."

"I understand that," replied the sergeant, "and you were not injured. I'll pass the information to Lt. Janczyn as soon as I can."

Geoff looked as unhappy as Jenna felt. He had mud streaks on his left cheek; his hair was awry, and his shirt was a mass of wrinkles. One sneaker was dry and white; the other sloshed as he walked and was color coordinated with the streaks on his face. Little puddles were collecting about his feet as gravity slowly pulled the water from his jeans.

Jenna had no idea what she looked like and refused to look in a mirror. What she didn't know couldn't embarrass her. She suspected that she looked worse than Geoff.

When she ran her hand through her hair and a gentle fall of dirt mantled her shoulders, she wasn't really surprised.

"There's one thing you *can* do while you wait to contact the lieutenant," Geoff said. "There are some spent shell casings at the bridge. I left them there because I assumed they were the evidence you would need to authenticate that a crime did indeed occur. Someone ought to go get them before something happens to them."

"There's also a shattered rock," added Jenna. "A flying piece of it cut me here." She stuck out her hand, noting without surprise that it was shaking.

The sergeant looked at her hand and nodded. "Don't worry," he said.

"Don't worry?" she repeated. "Someone tried to kill us! Again!"

The sergeant just looked unhappy. He obviously didn't like being yelled at because his superior was unavailable.

"I don't suppose there's any way you can arrange protection for Mrs. Mathisson and me, is there." Geoff made it a statement rather than a question.

"If you'd like to wait here until the lieutenant or the chief is free, you're welcome to do so. They could answer that question."

Jenna looked at the clock on the wall. 4:30.

"I can't wait, Geoff. I've got to get my car, make myself decent, and be at the church by 6:00."

He nodded. "Just tell the lieutenant we must see him," said Geoff.

As he drove her to East Edge Eddie's, he said, "I'll wait for you to get your car and follow you home."

"You don't have to do that," she protested automatically.

"Are you saying you don't want to hang around with me

any more because I'm too dangerous?"

She smiled at him. He was dangerous all right, but it had nothing to do with desperate killers.

Eddie was waiting for her when they reached the garage. "Hey, Mrs. Mathisson, I was getting worried."

"Thanks for waiting, Eddie," she said.

"What'd you do, fall into Stony Creek?" he asked as she got out of Geoff's car.

"Exactly." Jenna shook her leg and the still damp jeans sprinkled on Eddie's macadam.

"Sounds like fun," said Eddie. "Great weather for it."

Jenna offered him a tight smile as she paid the bill and left.

As she drove through town, she looked at her fuel gauge. Almost empty. She'd pull into Rolf's and get some gas.

Jenna looked in her rearview mirror. Geoff was right behind her. She signaled as she approached Rolf's and pulled up to the full service pumps at the island closest to the building. It might cost her a few cents more, but today she needed someone to pump her gas. Her knees felt a little too weak to hold her.

The station gleamed in the late afternoon sun; the new siding on the office and garage was shiny and white. Two islands directly in front of the office provided several selections of gas, either full-serve or self-serve. A large paved area to the right of the building housed the diesel pumps with their long, derrick-style arms. It all looked very prosperous, just like Harley had told her. The East Edge Chamber of Commerce, of which Rolf was a past president, must be proud.

Geoff followed her into the station but pulled on through and stopped by the exit so he wouldn't block any business. Almost immediately, two semis pulled in and circled around to the diesel pumps. A pick-up truck pulled up to the self-service island, blocking Geoff from view. But Jenna knew he was there, and that's what counted.

"Hey, Jenna. What can I do for you?" Harley Tester stood beside the car. He was the perfect height for the job. No bending necessary.

"Two dollars worth, Harley." That should be enough for the next few days if she were careful.

Jenna rested her head on the back of the seat as Harley filled the car. She was exhausted. But there was the recital to get through before she could think of sleep. And her dinner date with Geoff.

She straightened. Suddenly she wasn't so tired after all. Absently she watched an attendant helping the truckers fill their rigs. She looked at him more closely.

"Two dollars, Jenna," said Harley.

She passed a pair of ones through the window.

"Harley, who's that over there?" She indicated the other attendant. "I think I've met him."

Harley looked at Jenna. "That's Joby White. Where'd you ever meet him?"

"I thought so. I met him through one of my students. Is he a good worker? Do you like him?"

Harley shrugged. "He's sort of impetuous, you know what I mean? He overreacts. Has a bad temper. Takes off sometimes without telling me. Just leaves. He drives me nuts sometimes, too, because he thinks he knows it all. Hah! Wet behind the ears in spite of his record with the girls."

132

"Lots of girls?" asked Jenna.

"Lots," said Harley. "They try to hang around here, but I won't let them. One good thing about the kid—at least he shows up every day which is more than I can say for most of the guys Rolf hires."

Poor Thelma, thought Jenna. Her Joby was a faithless rat.

When Jenna pulled up to Geoff's car, he was resting his head on his seat just as she'd been doing, but he'd fallen asleep.

She suddenly felt panicky. Hadn't he?

"Geoff!" she called urgently through the open windows, "Geoff!"

He blinked, sat up, and grinned ruefully. "Some protector I am."

Grinning in relief at her needless fear, Jenna waved and pulled out of the station.

When they reached her house, Geoff waited in her drive until she went in and came back to tell him it was clear.

"Call me when you get home so I know you're all right," she said.

They looked at each other and laughed.

"This is ridiculous," he said.

"Absolutely," she agreed. "But call me anyway."

Jenna got ready in record time, undoubtedly because she had no one to dress but herself. She tucked a string of pearls under the collar of her rose dress and adjusted the rose and white belt Janie had given her for her birthday last year. She attached pearl studs to her ears and spent extra time with her makeup. She slipped on her white dress shoes and went to wait for Geoff.

When she opened the door to his knock, she realized how strange it seemed to see him dressed up. His gray slacks and navy blazer with a light blue shirt and cranberry foulard tie made him seem so impressive, so professional. *It was strange,* she thought, *how different clothes made you look like a different person.* Someday soon she must see him in his doctor's whites.

They drove straight to the church. As the recital started, everyone was nervous, the parents, the students, and the teacher. In fact, Jenna was certain the teacher felt the worst of all.

Still, everyone did very well in spite of the fact that Alex in white slacks and a navy blazer played his entire first number an octave too low.

"Alex," called Jenna softly from her seat on the first row.

He heard and looked at her just before he began *Summer Rain.*

"Move up, Alex. You're an octave too low. Look for Middle C."

Alex scowled at her a moment, then looked at his hands. He searched for Middle C, found it, and stayed right where he was. *Summer Rain* sounded more like a thunderstorm than a shower.

An obviously nervous Valerie in a new white dress was next. As Jenna smiled encouragingly at her, she settled herself, taking care to be certain Middle C was where it belonged, and began. *Minuet in G* danced stolidly through the air. As Valerie curtsied, her cheeks now flushed with relief, Rolf could be heard applauding extra-enthusiastically.

Finally Thelma approached the bench.

"Mommy," yelled Kareem. "Where you going?"

Everyone laughed, including Thelma. She looked lovely in a black dress that fell straight from the shoulders. Its large white collar was edged with lace and a red silk rose was fastened at the throat.

Fur Elise floated on the air, not perfectly played, but done with feeling for the music, that elusive emotional quality that most never master. Thelma had it without even knowing what it was.

Oh, Father, thought Jenna. *Don't let that talent go to waste! Bring her to you, Lord Jesus. Please.*

16

The sun was setting, duplicating its vibrancy on the mirror of the reservoir. As the dining room hostess showed Rolf's party to a table by a large window overlooking the reservoir, Jenna was glad it was summer solstice. It was nearing nine o'clock, but the view was still magnificent.

The club dining room was still quite full and many people called to Rolf. He stopped frequently to shake hands with the men and offer compliments to the ladies. Jenna studied him covertly for a few minutes.

"My dad's not the great guy you and everyone else think he is," Valerie had said not twenty minutes ago as she came into Jenna's house to watch Mikey and Libby. "He's a showman. He likes to impress people."

"Valerie," Jenna had said, distressed. "You know your dad is a fine man. He certainly cares for you and your brother. Lots of divorced dads hardly ever see their kids. Look at all the time he spends with you."

"If what we do is public," the girl said cynically. "He was very happy to go to Sean's game last night and my recital tonight. It makes him look good. But do you know how much time he has spent with just the two of us this weekend or any weekend? Only the time it takes to drive us where we're going."

Jenna was distressed that the girl saw her father in such a harsh light. Rolf was a thoughtful person.

"Are you upset because he volunteered you to babysit for me?" Jenna asked.

Valerie shrugged. "Who cares? I can watch TV here as well as at his house. Though I'd rather be with my mother. At least she talks to Sean and me."

Now at the club, Jenna watched Rolf glad-handing his way across the dining room. He was certainly a people person. It would be easy for someone like that to overlook how much his presence meant to his kids.

"You know," said Trish, "I haven't been out to eat in a place this fancy in a long time. In fact, the last time we ate out, we went to McDonald's."

Geoff looked at Trish closely as if to see if she were joking. But Jenna knew she wasn't.

Rolf took his seat and the ordering began.

"I want you all to have filet mignon," Rolf said. "You're my guests, and you must have the best."

The last rosy tint was fading from the sky as the appetizers arrived. The stars were visible here and there through an increasing cover of clouds.

Jenna attacked her onion soup with hunger. Now that the recital was over, she could relax. If, that is, no one else shot at her or Geoff, tried to push them off a cliff or made threatening phone calls.

Suddenly Trish sighed.

"Rolf, will you change seats with me? Every time I look

out the window, I think of Bobby Coe floating on the water."

"Don't worry," said Geoff as Rolf willingly complied with Trish's request. "Bobby wasn't in the water in this vicinity."

"He wasn't?" Trish looked a little happier.

"How do you know?" asked Sal.

Jenna looked at Geoff and raised an eyebrow. The lieutenant had urged silence. He raised his shoulders as if to say, "Why not tell? These people are friends. And the villians seem to know who we are anyway."

"I saw them dump the body," Geoff said.

Trish almost choked on her forkful of salad.

"You what?" asked Rolf, astonished.

"I was jogging late and happened on the men dumping the body. That's how I got this." He ran his finger along the scab on his head. "Obviously they missed doing me great damage, but not by much."

"He ran away from the men and passed out on my patio," said Jenna. "That's how we met."

Sal laughed and Trish hooted, "You're kidding! I thought Janie introduced you."

"I'm sure she'd have gotten around to it in short order," said Geoff. "We just beat her to it."

"Did you see anything important?" asked Rolf. "I mean, of course what you saw was important. But anything the police can use to locate the murderers?"

"Yes and no," said Geoff. "I saw one of the men in the light, but I was so sick and exhausted that I can't remember what I saw."

"And that's not all," said Jenna. "Last night we found a cache of drugs down at the reservoir."

She grinned at the expressions on everyone's faces.

"Jenna," said Rolf, slowly, deliberately, "you've gotten yourself into a terrible situation."

His solemn concern warmed her.

"I agree," she said. "But I didn't do it on purpose, you know. Besides, Geoff's in a worse situation than I am. I've seen no one. Unless you count the man who shot at us this afternoon, and that was only a silhouette."

"What?" Trish gave up on her salad. "Someone shot at you this afternoon?"

Jenna nodded. "Kept us pinned behind a rock."

Rolf couldn't help laughing. "You make it sound like a bad cowboy movie."

"Would that it were," said Geoff feelingly.

"Wait a minute," said Sal. "I'm thoroughly confused. I think you'd better start at the beginning."

As the waitress collected appetizer dishes and served the entree, Jenna and Geoff told their story.

"I didn't know when I invited you that you would entertain us with your own private mystery story," commented Rolf with a shake of his head when Jenna and Geoff finally finished. "Have you read ads and articles about hotels and resorts and even cruise lines having murder weekends? You know—where you go and try to solve a scripted murder that the establishment acts out for you. Your story beats all that by a mile."

"I don't know," said Geoff. "That kind of adventure sounds a lot safer."

"You're sure there's nothing you can tell the police?" Rolf asked.

"You sound like Lt. Janczyn," said Jenna.

"I've tried and tried," said Geoff, shaking his head, "but

nothing's coming back."

"Are the body and the drugs and the shooting and all the rest connected?" asked Sal. "I should think they have to be, wouldn't you?"

"I think so," said Geoff. "I find it hard to believe that we've stumbled into two or three or four hornets' nests at the same time. The question is—how are they connected?"

Sal finished the last bite of his filet. "You know, yesterday that bag man, Charlie Wino, accused me of using The Lighthouse as a front for distributing drugs. He knew I used to be a junkie, and he let me know he thought I was Bobby Coe's source."

"Charlie's our main suspect," said Jenna.

"Why's that?" asked Rolf.

"Nothing concrete," said Jenna. "He just doesn't ring true somehow."

"Maybe he's a narc," suggested Sal. "Though if he is, his cover has been very consistent. I don't know how he could stand to smell that way on purpose."

Rolf thought a moment. "I can see why someone might think The Lighthouse could be a cover," he said. "You maintain an open door policy, and all kinds of people come in and out the place. A mission would be a good front for a lucrative side business. It's probably hard for some people to believe you would change for your religion."

Sal looked offended that Rolf could even suggest the possibility that Charlie had a viable idea.

"You're not serious, Rolf, are you? After we've sweated and starved for three years, do you really think people suspect we're just fooling?"

"He's just kidding, Sal." Trish smiled at her husband, then sought to ease any possible conflict by changing the direction of the conversation slightly. She whispered conspiratorily to Rolf, "The secret actually involves me, not Sal. I am very greedy and want my husband's insurance money. I'm the mastermind behind the drugs, and I plan to discredit Sal by planting some coke in his office and then having him bumped off by what looks like a rival gang so I can collect all $10,000 of his insurance money."

Rolf laughed. "It's been done for less. Though personally I favor Geoff. We all know doctors have access to great masses of drugs. Geoff's been robbing the hospital store, and somehow Bobby found out and had to be silenced."

"No, Rolf," said Jenna. "It's you. You have the drugs delivered at your truck stop and distribute them through Harley. Bobby knew your identity, so you did him in."

"No, no, Jenna," said Sal. "It's you. You have all these people regularly arriving at your house for piano lessons, or so it is thought. Actually, you are supplying them with all the drugs they want."

"Even Alex?" asked Jenna.

"Even Alex's mother," said Geoff. "Especially Alex's mother."

The quintet laughed and speculated their way through coffee and dessert. When they finally finished, they were the only party still in the dining room. Rolf looked at his watch.

"It's almost 11:00," he said. "When there's no special occasion, the club closes about now. I guess we'd better go before they tell us to. While this evening's been special

142

to us, I doubt the club manager would see it the same way."

"It has been a great evening," said Sal. "Thanks."

Everyone murmured their appreciation as they wound their way through the empty tables.

"I haven't eaten this well in ages," said Trish. "I didn't realize the country club was such a nice place."

Rolf nodded. "I'm having a birthday party here for Val next Saturday," he said. "Boys and girls, a disc jockey, the whole teenage thing. I hope she likes it." He laughed. "I'm giving up an afternoon of golf, so she'd better."

Jenna felt certain Valerie would hate it. The quiet, reserved girl would probably rather have a few girlfriends over for a pajama party.

Trish and Jenna stopped for a minute to admire a massive bouquet of silk flowers by the main entrance.

"Come on, Trish. It's time to go," urged Sal, apparently uninterested in silk flowers.

Jenna, Geoff and Rolf followed the Narduccis to the door.

"Oh!" said Jenna as she spun around. "I left my shawl at the table."

"I'll get it," volunteered Geoff. He left and returned quickly with the flimsy wrap dangling from his hand.

Jenna walked toward him, hand extended.

"Thanks." She smiled up at him and was struck by the stupified look on his face.

He was staring at the front door. She turned to look but saw only Rolf and Harley, who had appeared from somewhere, talking and gesturing excitedly. She looked back at Geoff.

"What's wrong?" she asked.

"That's him, Jenna. Where's a phone?"

"That's who? And down the hall there toward the back door."

"The man who chased me," Geoff said. "That little guy! I knew there was something special about him, but for the life of me, I couldn't remember. But that's him!"

He grabbed her wrist and began dragging her down the hall toward the phone. Jenna threw a glance over her shoulder to the front door and saw Harley staring intently at Geoff's retreating back.

"He's looking at you, Geoff," Jenna said urgently. "I don't know if he recognizes you or not."

Geoff found the pay phone down a deserted hallway near a back entrance. He fished in his pocket for a quarter and dialed 0.

"I need the police right away," he told the operator. "This is an emergency!"

Jenna kept looking down the hall the way they'd come. She couldn't believe she was watching for Harley!

"It was Harley? You're certain?" she asked Geoff.

"If Harley's the little guy, I'm certain."

She nodded. "That's Harley Tester."

Someone rounded the corner and Jenna's heart jumped to her throat. Then she recognized Rolf.

"Oh, you startled me!" she told him.

"Sorry about that. In fact, I'm sorry about a lot."

"Lt. Janczyn," Geoff said into the phone. "Tell him it's Geoff McGregor with the name of the man who killed Bobby Coe."

Suddenly the door behind Geoff opened and walking in from the night came Harley. In his hand was a small silver gun. It was leveled at Jenna's stomach.

"Hang up!" ordered Harley. "Immediately!"

Geoff saw the gun and carefully replaced the receiver.

"This way." Harley pointed to the door by which he still stood. "Outside. And say nothing to anyone if you value her at all."

"Harley, what are you doing?" whispered Jenna.

"Shut up, Jenna. Just move. All three of you."

Jenna turned toward the door, Geoff behind her. Rolf brought up the rear.

We can't just walk off with this man, Jenna screamed silently to herself. *After all, there are three of us and one of him. And I used to like him! I let Mikey fish with him! I thought I was his friend!*

Jenna reached for the handle to the back door just as an office door halfway down the hall opened. The door read MANAGER.

A tall, beefy man stepped into the corridor and looked at the gathering by the back door in surprise. He approached them and stood immediately across from Harley.

"Well, hello there, folks. Good to see you. In fact, Rolf, you're just the man I wanted to see. I've been going through my calendar for next week, and I see you're having a party here for your daughter's birthday. But I have no idea what you want to feed all those kids. And if I have no idea, obviously the kitchen has no idea either."

Rolf smiled painfully at the manager. "I've been meaning to call you, Stan, and I keep forgetting."

Harley stood plastered against the wall, his gun held behind his back and out of view.

Geoff suddenly realized that Harley could do nothing in

145

front of Stan, and yanked the back door open in front of Harley. Grabbing Jenna by the hand, he stepped outside, pulling her after him.

"Come on, Jenna," he shouted. "Run!"

Together they angled off behind the clubhouse into the welcoming darkness of the golf course.

17

Geoff and Jenna ran unhesitatingly toward a row of evergreen trees that marked the edge of the first fairway. Behind that open stretch were more conifers, darkness, a fragile security, and, at the top of the hill, Janie and Arch's house, a telephone, and the police.

Jenna looked over her shoulder as they plunged between the trees and got a slash across the face from a branch. She rubbed at the pain distractedly. Of much greater concern was the sight of Rolf emerging from the building with Harley behind him, gun in hand.

Would Harley hurt Rolf?

"There they go!" Harley's voice rang in the quiet of the night.

Jenna followed Geoff as they burst from among the trees to cross the openness of the fairway. She felt very exposed and vulnerable in spite of the limited visibility. The clouds that had begun moving in at sunset now had the stars obliterated. But there were shades of gray and black, and certainly anyone looking for them would see them.

Racing across the soft grass, Jenna felt like she was running through molasses. She had had this feeling of things moving in slow motion in other times of crisis. Wasn't adrenalin supposed to pump you up, not slow you down?

Nagging at her was concern for Rolf. Maybe they should return to try and help him. But what could they do? They were powerless against a gun. Surely the best possibility was the police.

Engrossed in her thoughts, she didn't see the tee marker at the first tee until the last possible moment. She swerved to miss it, but the heel of her shoe caught in the sod, turning her ankle. She fell heavily.

Geoff reached out to her and pulled her to her feet.

"Are you all right?"

"I think so." It was hard to speak with the breath knocked out of her. "My shoe." She groped about in the darkness.

He shook his head. "No time."

"I got it!"

She jammed it on her foot and limped with him to a great sycamore tree that lay between the first and second fairways.

They threw themselves behind the mighty boll of the tree and peeked cautiously back the way they had come.

Nothing. The golf course was eerily empty. Silently Geoff and Jenna scanned the darkness. Maybe Harley wasn't chasing them after all. Maybe he had decided to try to escape. Jenna wondered if perhaps they should cautiously return to the clubhouse and phone from there. It was so much closer than Arch and Janie's. One thing was certain, they couldn't go near Jenna's house. Mikey, Libby and Valerie were there; the danger to them was too great to risk.

Geoff leaned toward Jenna and placed his mouth beside her ear. "Maybe the easiest thing would be for you to stay here while I go back to the clubhouse; it's the closest building."

He had hardly finished the whispered comment when all the lights surrounding the large white building were extinguished, plunging them shades deeper into the night.

Jenna could feel the tension in him as Geoff gripped her hand. "Oh, well," he said. "It's up the hill after all."

"But not without me!" Jenna hissed. "I'm not staying here alone!"

"You know," he said into her ear, "if you think this evening is exciting, wait until our next date."

"I don't know," she whispered back, "I don't think my heart can take much more of this riotous living. Let's become dull and stodgy."

She saw the white of his teeth as he smiled.

Turning uphill, they edged away from the protection of the tree and raced across the green, dodging the flag that marked the second cup as it unexpectedly loomed out of the darkness.

Suddenly the ground dropped from under Jenna's feet and she fell, stifling a scream as she landed on her back at a forty-five degree angle. She felt and heard Geoff hit the ground beside her with a dull thud. As she tried to pull herself achingly to her feet, fine, gritty soil yielded beneath her touch.

"We're in a sand trap!"

149

"Tell me," said Geoff as he spat sand.

Scrambling out of the trap, they raced through the line of trees that separated the second and third fairways. Lights from houses at the top of the hill beckoned, tantalizingly close.

The third fairway ran parallel to the first two until it doglegged to the left at yard 167. Hand-in-hand they raced across its pliant grass straight into a wall of water.

Jenna gasped, shocked, and inhaled a mouthful of water. She began to cough. Geoff sputtered unhappily under his breath as the sprinkler moved easily on.

A figure stepped out of the darkness.

"You folks certainly are easy to follow. You make more noise than a regiment of soldiers."

Jenna and Geoff, frozen by surprise, stared at Harley and the gun, still steady in his hand.

"I presume you recognized me back there," said Harley to Geoff.

"As soon as I saw you," Geoff answered deliberately. "I knew there was something distinctive about the figure I had seen, but I couldn't quite put a finger on it."

"I'm sorry you remembered. And I'm sorry Jenna was with you when you did. I honestly hate having to hurt either of you."

"Then don't," said Jenna urgently. "Killing us won't help, Harley. You can't possibly expect to escape." She wished her voice didn't sound so hopeless. "The manager saw us together, and Rolf will go to the police if he hasn't already."

"Rolf will not go to the police." Harley's voice was a flat and final statement.

"What have you done to Rolf?" Jenna cried. "What have

you done? He was your friend!"

"Shut up, Jenna!" Harley's voice was rough. "Now I want you two to march straight up the hill to the road."

The road! Steagers' house!

"And don't get any funny ideas about escape," Harley added. "I have a car waiting. I'll shoot you here if I need to, but I prefer to have you walk out under your own power. Now move."

He moved next to Jenna, on the far side from Geoff. His gun was pointed unwaveringly into the small of Jenna's back. There was no choice but to begin walking.

They had taken only a dozen steps or so when they walked into the wall of water again. The sprinkler had made its circuit and come back to them.

The water hit Harley as a complete surprise and in that split second, a man stepped from behind a large conifer and shouted, "That's it! Throw down your weapon! Police!"

Startled, Jenna recognized Charlie Wino. But it was not the derelict Jenna thought she knew. He was dressed the same, and he smelled the same, but there all resemblance to the hobo who trekked about town ended. This Charlie Wino stood tall and erect, a man of command and in command. The handgun he held furthered the impression of authority.

"Pick up Harley's gun, Dr. McGregor, please," said Charlie.

"Don't bother," a voice called out before Geoff could move. "I've got my gun pointed right at the lady."

Everyone spun around to see who was behind them.

"Joby!" said Jenna as the young man stepped forward. "What are you doing here?"

"Thanks, kid," said Harley as he disarmed Charlie Wino. "Great timing. Now let's all continue up the hill, if you please. But first, hands behind your heads!"

Feeling like she had fallen into Alice's rabbit hole, Jenna clasped her hands behind her head and walked beside Geoff as they trudged up the hill. She no longer knew the good guys from the bad guys. Harley had been willing to kill her! And Charlie Wino was almost the hero!

"Are you a cop or something?" asked Jenna of Charlie.

"Or something," said Charlie, "Drug Enforcement Agency undercover agent."

"Stop talking!" ordered Harley.

"A narc," said Joby scornfully, ignoring Harley. "He's a narc!"

"A narc," agreed Charlie. "It's better than being a dealer."

"But what are you doing here, Joby?" Jenna asked.

"He works with me," Harley said. "Sort of my assistant."

Joby snorted. "Assistant! Little man, we got equal status."

"I have a question for you, Joby," said Geoff. "Did you follow us from town either yesterday or today?"

"Yeah," the boy said defiantly. "Both times. What of it? I recognized you yesterday at Miz Coe's house. I got suspicious. What were you doing there of all places? I tried to find where you lived, but there's no Dr. McGregor in the phone book."

Jenna and Geoff exchanged glances. Joby was her threatening caller, too.

152

"Then today when you drove past the gas station, I seen you. Miz Mathisson blew her horn and you were right behind her. I followed you all right. I'm only sorry I missed. But I think I'm about to get a second chance."

The pleasure in his voice chilled Jenna.

"Why did you kill Bobby?" asked Charlie Wino.

"He was making noises about telling what he knew. Ever since he got religion, he'd been a problem."

"But why did you hide the drugs?" Charlie asked. "It was terribly risky to let them out of your possession."

"We didn't know who he was." Harley jerked a thumb at Geoff. "We didn't want to get caught by the cops or somebody with all that on us. So Joby hid it."

"He didn't do a very good job, did he?" mocked Charlie.

Harley snorted. "Putting it where a kid can find it. He obviously didn't do any better a job there than he did in killing these two."

"I did so hide them good," protested Joby. "I hid them under the bridge under rocks and weeds. I don't know how they got found. And you didn't do so good shooting the doctor in the first place."

"Amateurs," jeered Charlie Wino.

Jenna only half listened to the conversation. Something had been said in the last few minutes that was significant, but she couldn't quite put her finger on it.

"Listen to who's talking about amateur," said Harley. "You been hanging around East Edge for over a year, and I bet you still haven't got evidence that'll hold up in court."

"Guess again, Harley," answered Charlie. "I've got enough to put both of you away for a long time."

"Sure you do, cop! Sure you do."

A large copper beech tree loomed up between them and the road, its branches gracefully touching the ground.

"Everybody to the left of the tree," ordered Harley. "And no more talking."

Suddenly a heart-stopping scream tore the night, its fierceness amplified by the empty acres of golf course surrounding them.

Almost as one, they jumped and swung toward the sound just in time to see a figure fly through the air and tackle Joby about the waist. The two fell thrashing to the ground.

Joby's gun flew out of his hand and Harley, Geoff, and Charlie Wino all lunged toward it. Midway in his spring, Charlie changed directions and slammed full strength into Harley.

Pressing herself against the beech tree, Jenna recognized Sal Narducci struggling to wrestle down the panicking Joby. While Charlie and Harley were locked in a fight for Harley's gun, Geoff seized the opportunity to grab Joby's gun and turn it on the writhing figures.

Suddenly, two arms snaked out and grabbed Jenna around the mouth and waist, pulling her into the dark cave beneath the beech's foliage. Dragged out on the other side of the tree's cave, she was forced roughly up the hill and into a waiting car. When her captor ordered her to drive, it was all she could do not to laugh and cry

154

hysterically. Everything else these last two days had been frighteningly surrealistic. Why not this? For even in the dim light, she had no trouble recognizing her captor.

Rolf hadn't gone to the police. He was part of the drug ring.

18

Jenna stared at Rolf in disbelief. And suddenly she knew what had struck her as vital in the earlier conversation.

Harley had known that she and Geoff had found the drug cache. And there was no way he could have known unless he had been told. The only people who knew besides the police and Charlie Wino were those who had sat around the dinner table when she and Geoff metaphorically hanged themselves.

No wonder Harley had been so upset when Jenna had seen him at the country club door. He had probably been telling Rolf that the drugs were not where they were supposed to be. Rolf must have told him what had happened.

Rolf had to be the head of the ring. Rolf, Valerie's father. Rolf, the glad-hander. Rolf, the community pillar. Rolf, who brought supplies to the mission even as he sold drugs to those the mission was in business to help.

Jenna felt suddenly angry. She glared at Rolf.

"Don't waste your energy being angry with me," Rolf

said quietly. "We have a lot to do and just a few minutes to do it."

"I won't cooperate," Jenna declared.

"Of course you will," said Rolf matter-of-factly. "You want to live."

Jenna felt goose flesh run up and down her arms, and she knew he was right. Fleeting images of her children—and Geoff—rushed through her mind. She did want to live. And clearly, distinctly, she recognized both her fear and the ruthlessness of the man beside her.

"Drive us down the hill to your place, Jenna." Rolf held the gun in his lap, pointed steadily at her.

"My house?" Jenna felt panicky. "But the kids are there."

"They'll never know we've come," Rolf said. "All we want is your car. Your kids are long in bed and Val's probably asleep in front of the TV. If by some miracle she's still awake, she's in the family room at the other end of the house from the garage. She should never hear us."

In the driveway before Jenna's two car garage, Rolf climbed out of his Cadillac.

"I want you to park my car in the garage and get yours out. I will walk beside whatever vehicle you're driving so I can keep an eye on you. I don't think you want to risk causing problems that would attract the attention of the kids."

Jenna tried to think of something she could do without endangering the kids, but her mind felt mired in molasses. Silently she complied with Rolf's demands.

She parked his Cadillac where Tommy's Porsche had once sat, then backed the Escort out.

Suddenly a desperate idea surfaced.

158

"I've got to close the garage door," she said.

"Don't try anything. I'm watching," Rolf said as he stood, eagle-eyed, in the drive. "And hurry!"

She climbed out of the car still clutching her purse and shawl. She pulled down the garage door and walked back to the Escort.

Rolf opened the passenger door and climbed in as Jenna opened her door and slid into her seat.

Let this work, dear God, she breathed, *please, let it work.*

As she reached to shut her door, she let her shawl slip out of her hand onto the driveway.

Jenna backed her Escort out of the drive, taking care not to turn on the headlights until she was driving away. Let Rolf think it was because she didn't want to attract Valerie's attention. Let him never suspect about the shawl.

"Go to the Morgantown exit of the Pennsylvania Turnpike and head west," Rolf said. "They'll look for us in Philadelphia and New York, but we won't be there."

The trick had apparently worked. She tried to keep the elation from her voice as she asked, "Where are we going?"

Rolf looked at Jenna. "You don't want to know my plans."

Jenna blinked, then stared, wide-eyed, at him.

Rolf slumped against the passenger door, resting his head on the back of the seat. "If you move unexpectedly, Jenna, I'll know it. And I am not in a patient mood. I don't have much else to lose right now, and I'll do whatever I have to to protect myself. Not that I want to harm you; you've always been one of my favorite people. However . . . ."

159

Jenna, appalled and frightened by this stranger in the familiar form, shivered in the warm night. Looking straight ahead, she concentrated on her driving. At the entrance to the turnpike, Jenna pulled the ticket from the toll machine, and followed the deserted ramp west toward Pittsburgh.

Rolf seemed asleep in his corner, but she wasn't about to test him. It was easier not to have to deal with him. However, after they had traveled fifty or so miles, Jenna had to waken him.

"Rolf, we're almost out of gas."

He sat up, immediately alert.

"Where are we?" he asked.

"Approaching the rest stop at Lawn. I'll have to get gas. And I've got to use the ladies' room."

He nodded, then closed his eyes. But Jenna knew he was no longer asleep.

They parked in front of the restaurant at the rest stop. There were only four other cars in the lot.

"Remember I have my gun right here in my pocket," Rolf said. "No tricky stuff, Jenna. I'd hate for innocent people to get hurt because of your foolishness."

She nodded, and they entered the building. Straight ahead were the men's and women's rooms. To the right were the restaurant and a food bar. The restaurant was closed but three couples and a single man sat at the food bar.

Jenna walked to the women's room door with Rolf right behind her.

"Not so fast, Jenna," he said, grabbing her arm before she could go inside. "Stop out here. There may be someone in there."

They stood side by side leaning against the wall waiting.

No one entered or left either restroom over a five minute span.

"Okay," Rolf said. "I'm willing to wager that it's empty. I wouldn't want you meeting anyone in there and talking to them, now, would I?"

Jenna just looked at him, hopelessness in her eyes.

A small, sand-filled trash can stood between the two restroom doors. Rolf pushed the ladies' room door open and propped it ajar with the trash can.

"I'll just wait here for you," he said. "If anyone comes near, I'll tell them the room is being cleaned, and they have to wait a minute. Now hurry!"

Jenna entered the ladies' room and tried to think of something she could do to get away from Rolf. But there were no windows or undetected people. When she moved to wash her hands, she stared dismally at her reflection.

The idea was quick and exciting. She reached into her purse and grabbed her lipstick. In large, slashing letters she wrote across the mirror, "I'm a hostage! Help!" and signed her name.

"Jenna, do I have to come in and get you?" Rolf's low voice held a menacing threat.

"No!" she said too quickly. "No," she said again, heading for the door, hoping he took her distress for offended modesty.

They walked quickly to the car and drove to the service area.

"No funny stuff," Rolf said again as a sleepy looking attendant came to the window.

"Fill it," Jenna said. As he moved away, she turned to

Rolf. "Do you have money for this? I don't."

"Use a credit card," he ordered. "I'm not giving up cash for gas."

"What? You threaten my life, kidnap me, and now I have to pay for your getaway?" Indignation rang in her voice, but Rolf just laughed mockingly at her.

Jenna handed her credit card to the attendant who recorded her license plate number and gave her the receipt to sign. Feeling Rolf's eyes on her, Jenna wrote, "Call police!" instead of her name, stuffed her copy into her purse quickly and drove back out into the deserted night.

The turnpike unwound mile after dark mile. The clock on the dash showed two o'clock, then three o'clock. Harrisburg flew by and central Pennsylvania's farms and woods were black shadows at the road's edge.

"How did you ever get involved in something like drugs?" Jenna finally asked, unable to bear the silent, intimidating figure beside her anymore. "It doesn't make sense to me. You're too nice."

Rolf's sardonic smile flashed briefly in the dim, reflected light of the dashboard. "Money," he said succinctly.

"Money? But you have plenty! Your business is booming, and you're making a killing in the stock market."

"Now," he agreed, seemingly willing to talk. "But not always. Not always. A few years ago I was in debt to my ears over investments that went sour. I needed money fast. Harley was the one who suggested how lucrative dealing drugs could be."

Rolf laughed a short, harsh bark. "He'd just come back from visiting his family in New York, and he couldn't get

162

over how much money his brother had. He decided that if his brother, who Harley says has the brains of a nit, could make so much, we could really do well."

"And the truck stop is the perfect place, isn't it?" asked Jenna. "So many people coming and going. Deliveries would be easy and no one would ever suspect a thing."

"When you suggested that earlier this evening at dinner, I almost choked," said Rolf. "I couldn't figure out how you could possibly know."

"I didn't. It was just part of the general silliness."

Jenna drove in silence for awhile. The gas gauge read half empty. Occasionally another car caught up to them and passed, but they were primarily alone on the road.

"Don't you feel guilty about ruining people's lives?" Jenna suddenly asked, breaking into the desolate sounds of the road noise. "That's the part I'm having such a hard time reconciling."

Rolf snorted. "The way I see it, those people are going to ruin their lives whether I sell them the drugs or someone else does. I might as well be the one who profits from their stupidity."

"But what about Valerie and Sean?"

"What about them?" Rolf's voice was suddenly very cold. She had apparently hit on a sensitive topic.

"Don't you think it will hurt them to have a dad who's a crook?"

"A dad who's a successful crook," Rolf replied. "That's the difference. But if it hadn't been for you and the good doctor, they'd probably never have known."

Wisely Jenna kept silent. She didn't know whether he really believed that or just wanted to believe it. Any way she looked at it, the consequences of his actions would be devastating to his kids.

The Breezewood, Bedford and Somerset exits came and went. The tunnels were eerie as they drove through, the sole car in the vast amber lighted passageways. As the miles from East Edge grew, Jenna's anxiety grew.

'Be anxious for nothing.' 'Be anxious for nothing.' The Bible verse sprang into her mind and she repeated it over and over to herself. *'I will never leave you nor forsake you.'*

"What are you going to do with me?" Jenna finally asked, afraid to know—and afraid not to know.

"Drop you by the road in the middle of nowhere," Rolf replied easily, quickly."

"You're not—not going to kill me?"

He looked at her and grinned. "What do you think?"

"I honestly don't know." Jenna gripped the wheel and noted the gas gauge dropping lower and lower. "Yesterday I would have said you couldn't hurt anyone. Obviously I would have been wrong. If I didn't really know you yesterday, I certainly can't begin to understand what you're thinking today."

"Want to come with me, Jenna?" Rolf reached over and placed his hand on hers as it held the steering wheel. "I brought you along because I needed a hostage, but I'd rather take you willingly. I'd even marry you. We could make a fabulous life for ourselves."

It was all Jenna could do not to cringe under his touch. As it was, he felt her rejection without her saying a word. He laughed unpleasantly and removed his hand.

"Don't say I never offered you the world," he snapped.

"Rolf, give yourself up," Jenna pleaded. "Don't try and run. Where could you ever go and be safe? Especially if you kill me?"

Rolf shook his head. It suddenly hit Jenna that she could see him quite clearly. The sky was gently lightening. The dashboard clock said 4:30.

"I can't tell you where I'm going, but I expect to be quite happy. Suffice it to say that I'll be safe and sunny with a new name."

Jenna looked at him. "You're really prepared, aren't you?"

He nodded. "Of course. I've thought long and hard and planned very thoroughly," he said smugly. "It was always possible I'd have to leave my comfortable little set-up quite quickly."

"Squirreled your money away in a safe place?"

"In safe places, plural. Not all in one basket."

"I hate to present you with a new problem, but we need gas again. The New Stanton rest stop is coming up."

"So pull in and fill up," he said. "Then I'll drive."

Jenna's stomach clutched. He was planning to drop her soon. He must be. Dead or alive?

To distract herself from the thought, she asked, "Why did you come to the top of the golf course after we ran away tonight? You could have left immediately, and no one would have realized you were missing for a long time. And you wouldn't have needed to drag anyone along with you."

Rolf smiled benevolently at her. "I didn't trust Harley or Joby to finish off you and your doctor. They had made too many mistakes already. And obviously I was right. I just didn't know that there was an extra man wandering around to complicate things. I also never thought Sal would show up."

Headlights from a car that had been behind them for a little while pulled up to them, and then the car sailed by on the left. Jenna glanced over and felt little sparks explode all over her body. She shook her head. She must be hallucinating. The car disappeared rapidly over the horizon.

Soon the New Stanton rest stop appeared and Jenna drove up the ramp into the area. It was pearly light by now and numerous cars were parked in the restaurant area.

"Go right to the gas pumps," Rolf said. "No restroom this time."

Jenna pulled up to the pump. The yawning attendant peered in the window at her.

"Fill it up, please," she said wearily, suddenly feeling exhausted. She'd been driving for over five hours.

"Walk around to the passenger side," Rolf said. "And remember, I'm watching you."

"I have to sign for the gas, then I'll walk around."

"Walk around now," he commanded. "I'll pass you the receipt."

Feeling she had no choice, Jenna opened her door and stepped out. She wouldn't be able to leave a message on the receipt this time. Angrily she slammed her door and turned, bumping into the attendant.

"Sorry," she started to say when she realized that she hadn't bumped into the attendant at all. Rather he had grabbed her and was dragging her to the rear of the car and behind an eighteen-wheeler that suddenly appeared on the other side of the gas island.

In disbelief she watched as two attendants at the next island and the passenger in the truck rushed her car. Each of them held a gun trained right at the windshield and Rolf. Not a shot was fired as they pulled him from the car.

"Jenna!"

Jenna spun around and ran across the tarmac to Geoff who met her halfway.

"It *was* you in that car!" she sobbed on his neck. "Thank God, it was you!"

19

"I still can't believe it," said Janie Steager two weeks later. "We go away for a couple of weeks and you all go crazy. Breaking up drug rings. Getting shot at. Being held hostage."

Janie sat beside Arch on Jenna's patio waiting for the hamburgers to cook. Her tanned face with its peeling nose gave evidence of two weeks at the shore. She looked at the Narduccis.

"How did you two get drawn into all this?"

"Very peripherally," said Sal. "We just called the cavalry to the rescue."

"Don't be modest, Sal," said Jenna. "You saved the day with your flying tackle."

Janie looked blankly from one to the other.

Trish began explaining. "We had gone to dinner with Jenna and Geoff and Rolf at the country club. We spent the evening hearing all about Jenna and Geoff's adventures.

"It was 11:00 by the time we finished and left. When we were pulling out of our parking place at the back of the parking lot, though, we saw Geoff and Jenna run out the back door of the building and onto the golf course. A minute later Rolf and Harley came tearing out. Harley yelled, 'There they go!' and took off after them."

Sal leaned forward in his chair. "I knew something was dreadfully wrong, so I told Trish to go call the cops while I followed Jenna and Geoff."

"He took off before I could even argue," Trish said. "Then all the lights went out, and I saw Rolf race out to his car and drive away. It seemed like I banged on the door forever before Stan let me in to use the phone."

Jenna passed the hors d'oevres around.

Trish continued. "As soon as I called the station and mentioned Geoff's name, the police were interested. He had called them just a few minutes earlier, but they had no idea where from. He'd been cut off."

"What was going on up the hill while Trish was getting the police?" asked Arch.

"The Keystone Cops, if you ask me," said Jenna. "First Harley had us. Then Charlie Wino had him. Then Joby had Charlie. Then Sal attacked Joby. While they're all rolling around on the ground and Geoff's trying to figure out who he can shoot, if anyone, Rolf grabbed me. It sounds funny now, but I've never been more terrified in my life."

Trish put down her iced tea so she could use both hands to talk. "When the police arrived at the clubhouse, they questioned the club manager and learned that Geoff, Jenna, Rolf and another man, a little person, had been talking with him by the public telephone just before he closed. He had been struck by the strange behavior of Geoff and Jenna when they ran out the door so abruptly. Then Rolf and the little man, Harley, were just as abrupt.

He heard Harley yell, 'There they go!' but thought nothing of it. He said people are always playing weird jokes on each other, and he figured this was just another."

"Some joke!" said Janie with a shudder.

Trish grinned. "The police were all ready to begin this immense search of the golf course when who should walk out of the shadows but Harley and Joby with their hands up. Behind them was Charlie—real name, Sgt. Jack Palmer—with a gun in each hand. Next came Sal and Geoff yelling for Jenna at the top of their voices because she'd disappeared."

"Sgt. Palmer," said Jenna slowly. "I still have trouble calling him anything but Charlie Wino. He came here last week to visit Mikey. He wanted Mikey to see him as he really is, not remember him as Charlie Wino. Mikey loved it. Now he wants to be an undercover cop when he grows up." Jenna held her head. "Just the nice safe career every mother wants for her son."

Geoff grinned, walked to the grill and flipped the hamburgers. "We're just about ready here."

Eventually the five kids were all served and settled around a large plastic tablecloth thrown on the lawn, though how much they would actually eat was an open question. The adults left them to their own devices.

"Any spills, you mop them up," warned Janie.

"No problem," agreed Mikey. "We'll just pour them into the grass."

The picnic table had been placed in the shade for the adults and was laden with contributions from Trish and Janie as well as Jenna. Everyone was served before Janie went back to the topic that was still uppermost in her mind.

"Okay, so you guys figured out Jenna was missing. What did you do then?"

"That was all Geoff's doing," said Trish.

Everyone looked at Geoff expectantly.

"No big deal," he said modestly. "I wanted to make certain the kids were all right and wondered if possibly, for some crazy reason, Jenna might have gone to her house—maybe to call the police. So I had Lt. Janczyn bring me here to Jenna's. Lying in the driveway was her white shawl, the very one I had gotten for her in the dining room at the club that evening. She *had* been at the house, and then in the garage we discovered Rolf's Cadillac, not her little car. Bingo, we knew what car to look for—and who was with her."

He smiled at Jenna. "Of course, she helped herself in the women's room at the first rest stop by writing HELP all over the place like the wonderful woman she is."

Jenna blushed under his praise. "I've always wondered what the first woman to enter the ladies' room thought when she saw that message. I'm not certain what I would have thought if I were the one who found it. Is it real? Is it a joke? And I worried about the attendant noticing the message on that gas receipt. He looked ready to fall asleep on his feet."

"Bet your note woke him up fast," said Trish.

"I guess both messages got reported to the night manager because he's the one who called the state police to report them," said Geoff. "The state police in turn had received the APB concerning Rolf kidnapping Jenna. A simple matter of two plus two. Now they knew where he and Jenna were."

"But how did they know where Rolf would go? How did

they know where to set up their trap?"

"The big problem was establishing whether he was still on the turnpike. If he was still on that road, they could track him because the interchanges are so far apart. They put unmarked cars on at all of them to see if they could locate the Escort. They found it between Breezewood and Somerset and followed it from that point. They knew approximately how soon the Escort would need more gas and the limited number of rest stops simplified matters greatly."

"You almost didn't make it," Jenna said, remembering how close to New Stanton they had been when Geoff and the police passed her.

He nodded. "But the state police would have been waiting whether we made it or not. The only reason Lt. Janczyn was there was because I was going to go whether he went or not. After all, if it weren't for me, you wouldn't have been in that situation to begin with. I think he was afraid I'd wreck the whole setup.

"We began driving west long before you were spotted. But it was a dangerous game of 'Catch-Up.' We kept in touch with what was going on by police radio. I must say, though, that I've never driven such speeds in my life and I never want to again!"

Everyone munched hamburgers and salad in silence as they contemplated Geoff's wild dash across the state.

Arch broke the silence. "I've one question. How did Rolf plan to escape?"

Jenna smiled sadly. "He had developed a second identity in case his operation here ever failed. He had a wallet on him full of cards identifying him as Randall J. Whitman. He even had a passport. I don't know how he got all those papers, but he did. He even had most of his money in bank accounts in the Whitman name. He was going to fly out of Pittsburgh as Whitman and set himself up in the Caribbean."

"Unbelievable," said Sal, shaking his head. "Unbelievable."

"I feel so badly for Valerie and Sean," said Jenna. "I keep thinking how devastating it must be to have your father splashed all over the newspapers. And they're extra vulnerable being in that early adolescent group."

"Poor Thelma's having a hard time, too," said Trish. "She's taking it badly about Joby. She thought he was her knight-in-shining-armor. She's always at the mission now, playing the piano to ease her hurt. I'm about to go crazy! But I'm also praying and biding my time. There'll be lots of opportunities for me to talk with her eventually."

Dessert was Janie's special ice cream cake made with lots of chocolate, whipped cream, and mint ice cream. The kids inhaled it and wanted more.

"Go play," said Arch. "The rest is mine."

"Uncle Arch!" exclaimed Libby, appalled that he'd keep all that for himself.

"I'll share it with the other adults," he said at her shocked expression.

Mollified, she ran to join the others in climbing trees. She and Patsy ended up sitting on a stump and giggling while Tim, Zach and Mikey played Tarzan.

"Do you know what bothers Janie the most about all this?" asked Arch. "She never got the chance to introduce Geoff and Jenna."

"Oh, Arch, shush up," said Janie, irritated enough to prove what he said was true.

Arch nodded. "She's been planning her moves ever since she knew Geoff was coming to East Edge. And you know she was serious, Jenna, because she never leaked a word of it to you, did she?"

Jenna had no idea how to respond and was relieved when the beeper on Geoff's hip sounded.

"Are you aware that a rare and beautiful thing has happened this evening?" Geoff said as he stood. "I got through a whole meal without being paged. Excuse me."

He went toward the patio door and Jenna followed him with her eyes. There was no question that he was a special person. There was also no question that she was attracted to him, and he seemed to return the favor. But they both needed time, time filled with normal pursuits and normal activities, to see if the affection that had bloomed under great stress could withstand the strain of everyday life.

He must have felt her eyes on him because he turned and smiled before going inside.

She grinned back. It seemed to her that he would prove to go very well, indeed, with everyday life.